"Oh, my!" cried _____ ght of the Duke of Litt_____ ing carriage."

"It is a curricle," the duke corrected her.

"Oh, no," she said. "It is a magic carpet." She picked up her skirt and ran down the front walk.

He smiled and strolled after her. It was a fine equipage. At least the girl had discriminating taste in something.

Once handed up, Miss Brightham sat beside him in silence, looking about. Oddly refreshing to find a lady who didn't jabber at one constantly, thought Littlefield.

As if feeling his gaze upon her, Betsy turned her head and smiled at him—that sunny, mischievous smile. "I suppose I should say something witty and entertaining to you. But, truth to tell, I haven't the least notion what to say to amuse a duke," she confessed.

"Tell me about your life," suggested Littlefield.

"Oh, that would surely not entertain you," she said, shaking her head. "Shall I tell you, instead, what I would like my life to be?"

"If you wish," said Littlefield.

"I should like to travel the world—be a lady explorer . . ."

The rest of the drive passed pleasantly, more pleasantly than the duke could have imagined, in fact. And as they pulled up in front of his grandmother's town house, he found himself feeling oddly sad to see their time together come to an end. 'Tis a pleasant game I'm playing, he told himself, sizing up Miss Brightham and seeing how I can pass her off as quality. I simply hate to end the game so early today. That is all I am feeling. Nothing more . . .

ZEBRA REGENCIES
ARE
THE TALK OF THE TON!

A REFORMED RAKE (4499, $3.99)
by Jeanne Savery

After governess Harriet Cole helped her young charge flee to France — and the designs of a despicable suitor, more trouble soon arrived in the person of a London rake. Sir Frederick Carrington insisted on providing safe escort back to England. Harriet deemed Carrington more dangerous than any band of brigands, but secretly relished matching wits with him. But after being taken in his arms for a tender kiss, she found herself wondering — *could* a lady find love with an irresistible rogue?

A SCANDALOUS PROPOSAL (4504, $4.99)
by Teresa DesJardien

After only two weeks into the London season, Lady Pamela Premington has already received her first offer of marriage. If only it hadn't come from the *ton's* most notorious rake, Lord Marchmont. Pamela had already set her sights on the distinguished Lieutenant Penford, who had the heroism and honor that made him the ideal match. Now she had to keep from falling under the spell of the seductive Lord so she could pursue the man more worthy of her love. Or was he?

A LADY'S CHAMPION (4535, $3.99)
by Janice Bennett

Miss Daphne, art mistress of the Selwood Academy for Young Ladies, greeted the notion of ghosts haunting the academy with skepticism. However, to avoid rumors frightening off students, she found herself turning to Mr. Adrian Carstairs, sent by her uncle to be her "protector" against the "ghosts." Although, Daphne would accept no interference in her life, she *would* accept aid in exposing any spectral spirits. What she never expected was for Adrian to expose the secret wishes of her hidden heart . . .

CHARITY'S GAMBIT (4537, $3.99)
by Marcy Stewart

Charity Abercrombie reluctantly embarks on a London season in hopes of making a suitable match. However she cannot forget the mysterious Dominic Castille — and the kiss they shared — when he fell from a tree as she strolled through the woods. Charity does not know that the dark and dashing captain harbors a dangerous secret that will ensnare them both in its web — leaving Charity to risk certain ruin and losing the man she so passionately loves . . .

Available wherever paperbacks are sold, or order direct from the Publisher. Send cover price plus 50¢ per copy for mailing and handling to Penguin USA, P.O. Box 999, c/o Dept. 17109, Bergenfield, NJ 07621. Residents of New York and Tennessee must include sales tax. DO NOT SEND CASH.

Bringing out Betsy
Sheila Rabe

ZEBRA BOOKS
KENSINGTON PUBLISHING CORP.

For Jonesy

ZEBRA BOOKS are published by

Kensington Publishing Corp.
850 Third Avenue
New York, NY 10022

First Printing: December, 1994

Printed in the United States of America

One

"I beg your pardon?" said the duke, sure he could not have heard correctly the first time.

"I said," repeated his grandmother, "that I wish you to assist me in bringing out a young lady."

The Duke of Littlefield looked at his grandmother as if she had taken leave of her senses. What business was it of his to help with young ladies' come-outs? That was for females.

"I know very well what you are thinking," said Mrs. Whitworth. "And bringing out young ladies may very well be considered strictly a woman's concern, but in this case it is not. I wish vouchers for her to Almack's, and I want you to sponsor her come-out ball at Littlefield House."

Littlefield's mouth dropped open. How had such a thing befallen him?

Actually, he knew quite well how such a thing had befallen him. He was a man with little fortune left. His maternal grandmother was his only hope for the future. And they both knew it.

Not that Mrs. Whitworth held this fact over his head very often, for she loved her scapegrace grandson. And he could hardly be blamed for the fact that his father had been a rake and a gambler, and lost over half the family's fortune.

For only an instant, regret sat on her shoulder. Why she and the colonel had ever allowed their daughter to marry such a one! All for a title. Much good it had done the poor girl. All those years trying to produce an heir. Those many miscarriages. And when they finally did get their Littlefield heir, what did the duke do but get both himself and Mrs. Whitworth's poor, foolish daughter killed in a curricle accident before the lad was even of age.

No wonder Lionel was wild and a bit spoilt. With a paternal grandmother such as that flighty dowager duchess to guide him, the poor child hadn't a prayer. His grandmother Whitworth was the only one in his life with any sense. And the only one who could really manage him. He always got round his other grandmama with that charming smile and few well-chosen flatteries. But not this grandmother. It was she who called the tunes, by heaven. And when she called the tune, her grandson danced.

And now it was plain she was calling a tune her grandson did not like. "There is no sense looking at me in that manner, young man," she said. "For my mind is quite made up.

"Very well," said Littlefield. "You are most welcome to use the townhouse. And I shall have Grandmother Hopewell procure a voucher."

Mrs. Whitworth smiled and nodded regally. "That is most kind of you," she said. "And, of course, I shall expect you to be on hand at all the important occasions to lend countenance to Betsy."

"Betsy, is it?" scoffed the duke. "Sounds like a name for an upstairs maid."

"It is short for Elizabeth," said Mrs. Whitworth irritably. "And I can assure you the gel is a proper young lady and not an upstairs maid."

"How proper?" countered the duke.

"Proper enough," snapped his grandmother. "She was gently born and raised and attended Miss Marrywell's Seminary for Young Ladies."

"Ah," said the duke in the most perturbingly knowing fashion.

"What, pray, does that mean?" demanded Mrs. Whitworth.

A smile hovered at the corners of the duke's mouth. "Is that not the same seminary you attended?" he guessed.

"It is," said Mrs. Whitworth defensively. "And a very good one it is, too. Elizabeth's grandmother and I were there together."

Cits and nobodies, thought the duke, reflecting his paternal grandmama's values. "Mrs. Whitworth," she had often said, "smells of the shop."

Mrs. Whitworth had always been quick to point out to any who cared to listen that the smell had not been so offensive as to keep the Hopewells from marrying Whitworth money. She fixed her grandson with a stare which plainly dared him to speak ill of either the seminary or her old friend.

The duke wisely did neither. Instead, he returned to the subject of the mysterious Betsy. "Does this Betsy have a surname?" he asked.

"It is Brightham," said his grandmother.

"The Brighthams of?"

"I am sure you would not know them," replied Mrs. Whitworth huffily, her cheeks turning slightly pink. "And I would thank you not to play off those highborn airs with me, young man. It is most unbecoming."

Littlefield frowned. His grandmother was hedging; not a good sign. Lending the use of his opulent townhouse for a ball was bad enough, but being seen all over town with this unknown girl was quite a horse of another color. He had no desire to have his name linked with that of some little nobody fresh from nowhere. "I don't see why you should need me dancing attendance on the chit," he said.

"Oh, I am sure if you think about it you will see exactly why I need you dancing attendance on her," said Mrs. Whitworth sweetly.

A new horrible thought dawned on Littlefield. Did his grandmother, perhaps, nourish fond hopes of seeing this granddaughter of an old friend married to her grandson? He shuddered inwardly. Relatives of old friends were always plain. "What does she look like?" he asked suspiciously.

"Now, how should I know?" retorted Mrs. Whitworth, irritated afresh. "Her grandmother writes that she is quite lovely."

"Naturally," said Littlefield cynically.

Mrs. Whitworth grimaced. "Her looks can be of no concern to you," she said. "You are merely required to lend countenance to Betsy and use your position to see her properly launched into society."

The duke frowned. He detested being used. He detested having to squire about unknown young ladies. And he detested being a slave to his grandmother's every whim. He stiffened in his chair, an action not lost on Mrs. Whitworth.

"Of course," she said, studying the rings on her fingers, "I could always leave my fortune to the Ladies' Society for the Friends of Orphans. Or to Betsy, herself, for that matter, if she is unable to make a suitable match."

There was a moment's silence as will strained against will. Littlefield was the first to give. "I shall, of course, be happy to assist you in bringing out Miss Bright-cap," he said, looking anything but happy.

"Brightham," corrected Mrs. Whitworth, and beamed on her nephew.

Littlefield took leave of his grandmother and raced his curricle home, scowling all the way.

At Littlefield House he was short with the servants and did no justice to the fine meal on which his cook had labored so hard all afternoon. What did his grandmother mean by doing this to him? She obviously wished to make him a laughing-stock. And whom did she intend to invite to this come-out ball for Miss Birdham, or Bingham, or whatever her name was? The duke supposed his grandmother would ex-pect him to invite all the Hopewells' acquaintance, as hers consisted primarily of cits and gently bred nobodies from Miss Marrywell's Seminary for Young Ladies. Faugh! He had other plans for the season besides dancing attendance on a chit fresh from some seminary. What would his friends say?

She had a squint, the duke was sure. Or her face was pockmarked. He looked at his own handsome face in the looking glass as his valet readied him for an evening on the town. At twenty-five, Lionel Endymion Hopewell, fifth Duke of Littlefield, was a fine specimen of manhood. Granted, he was a bit of a rake. But it didn't make him any less desirable as a husband. He was titled, it was well-known that he had the most excellent of expectations, and he was heart-meltingly handsome. He had a fine strong chin with a dimple in the middle of it, a straight nose, and a firm mouth—not too thick, not too thin, just right. He had hazel-colored eyes fringed with lashes any young lady would be proud to own. Topping this Adonis-like face were reddish gold, curling locks, the kind ballet dancers and fair Cyprians longed to run their fingers through. And the body beneath the handsome head was no less perfect. Littlefield tried to imagine his perfect self accompanying a little drab of a thing

all about town, squiring her to balls and
routs. Ugh. Disgusting!

Curse it all! If it weren't for the fact that
his grandmother had all the money, he'd
tell her to find herself another bird for the
plucking and not the Duke of Littlefield.

The duke sighed. Naturally, he was fond
of the old girl. And he was always willing
to fulfill any reasonable request she might
make. But this was ridiculous! And a curst
nuisance, too.

Well, he'd get his grandmother Hopewell to smuggle the girl into Almack's, and
his grandmother Whitworth and her old
friend could decorate his house with every
potted palm and bolt of fancy cloth they
could find in London and fill the place
full of curious gawkers for the chit's come-
out, all with his blessing. But his grandmother had best not expect him to dance
with the girl, for he wasn't coming within
a foot of her!

"That woman!" declared the dowager
duchess after the duke had recounted his
visit to his other grandmother. "She honestly expects you to sponsor this . . . child?
Well, I hope you told her exactly how you
felt."

Her grandson squirmed. "Not exactly," he said.

The dowager duchess stared at him. "Lionel. You must be jesting," she said.

Littlefield smiled weakly.

Her Grace put a hand to her plump breast. "Oh," she said faintly. "Oh, Lionel. What have you done?"

"I?" cried Littlefield, insulted. As if it had been his idea to foist this unknown upon the ton!

"How could you have let her talk you into such a thing?" demanded his grandmama. She stretched out a plump arm to search among the bottles which sat on the small table next to her chair. "Where is my hartshorn?" she demanded in a tremulous voice.

The duke plucked the desired bottle from the collection. "What could I have done?" he argued. "After all, it is within her power . . ."

"Don't be ridiculous," snapped the dowager, pulling the stopper from the bottle with amazing vigor for such a frail creature. "She has been using that threat upon you for years. I am surprised it has any sting left at all."

The duke was truly insulted now. "Why on earth else would I agree to such a curst stupid thing?"

"Lionel, please. Your language."

"Sorry," muttered Littlefield. He fell silent. Why, indeed, had he allowed his grandmother to talk him into this? After all these years her threats of disinheritance held no more menace than a toothless dog. Or did they? The very idea of being destitute and having to marry a cit was horrible, unthinkable.

The Dowager Duchess of Littlefield sighed. "I suppose you shall have to go along with this."

"Will you procure me a voucher, then?" asked the duke hopefully.

"We shall see," she replied noncommittally.

And with that he had to be content. And with that, he told himself, his grandmother Whitworth would have to be content as well.

But she wasn't. "What do you mean you are not sure?" she demanded when again he sat in her drawing room.

The duke squirmed, wishing he had not obeyed her summons, wishing he had sent his excuses—sick, out of town, anything would have been preferable to sitting there feeling like a schoolboy caught in a prank. "I was unable to get a firm commitment from Grandmother Hopewell. She merely said, 'We shall see.' "

Mrs. Whitworth bit her lip. She looked pleadingly at her grandson. "Lionel, this means a great deal to me."

She sat regarding him with those little blue eyes, looking so small and frail. Who was proof against such rare humility? Littlefield smiled encouragingly at the old woman and patted her hand. "We shall get those vouchers. Don't you worry."

"The child comes next week," fretted Mrs. Whitworth.

"And we shall be ready for her," predicted the duke, then wondered whatever had possessed him. Next the old girl would be thinking he actually wished to help her with this ridiculous scheme. Even now she was looking at him as if his coat were made of highly polished armor. He scowled and took his leave.

The following week Littlefield called at Mrs. Whitworth's townhouse, ready to meet the squinting, pockmarked horror which his grandmama wished to foist onto polite society.

His grandmother's butler, wearing a look even more sober than usual, took his hat and gloves. "What's this, Johnston?" said the duke. "You look as if you have lost your last friend on earth."

"I beg Your Grace's pardon," said the butler, his face a mask of stone. "It must be something I ate."

There was a thundering noise of running feet on the landing above, and the duke looked at the butler in surprise. "Good God! What was that?"

The butler looked pained and opened his mouth to speak, but before he could, a whoop echoed down to them, followed by a small form sliding down the banister.

The little boy climbed off it and cocked his head, surveying Littlefield. "Are you the duke?" he asked. "I thought you would be old. Mrs. Whitworth is old."

Littlefield looked inquiringly at the butler.

"It is Master Andrew, Miss Brightham's brother," said Johnston.

Littlefield stared at the butler. His grandmother had merely mentioned a young lady. How many more of them were there? He felt a tugging on his pantaloons and looked down in horror at the dirty little hand clutching the cloth.

"Why aren't you old like Mrs. Whitworth?" asked the child.

"Because Mrs. Whitworth is my grandmother," said the duke.

The child looked perplexed. "I thought

only little boys had grandmothers," he said.

The duke smiled at this. "Little boys grow up, he said. "One is never rid of grandmothers."

The child digested this. "I am glad," he announced. "I like my granny. She tells me stories. Granny said if I was nice to you I could have a biscuit."

"I shall tell your granny that you were nice to me," promised the duke.

With a whoop of excitement, the child ran off down the hallway, and Littlefield could hear him calling for Cook.

"If Your Grace would care to wait in the drawing room?" suggested the butler.

"Yes," agreed Littlefield faintly. "I hope she has a good Madiera waiting for me."

"Indeed, she does, Your Grace," said the butler in sympathetic accents.

Littlefield entered the drawing room and went straight for the wine decanter, making himself at home and pouring a glass. He took a deep, fortifying drink. Well, a child was not so bad. One needn't see much of a child. That was what nurses were for. And the little fellow was actually rather likable.

A loud belch startled him into turning around. There, in a corner, sitting quietly was a crone in a lace cap. She smiled at him and chuckled. "You be a handsome morsel," she informed him.

The duke staggered back into the nearest chair. "Thank you," he said weakly.

At that moment his grandmother entered the room, preceded by a plump woman with coarse features and hair an alarming shade of red. His eyes widened, and he took another gulp of wine before rising.

"Maisy, allow me to present my grandson, the Duke of Littlefield," Mrs. Whitworth was saying.

"Oh, Your Grace," gushed the woman, and for a moment Littlefield feared she would rush him and embrace him. But after a few excited steps, she remembered herself and fell into a graceless curtsy.

"This is Mrs. Long," said his grandmother. "She has accompanied her granddaughter to London and plans to stay for the season."

They took their seats, and Mrs. Long set out to explain her presence to the duke. "Yes," she said, nodding. "I thought to myself, wouldn't it be delightful to see my dear old friend after all these years. And such a treat for Andrew to see London. Of course, you have not met little Andrew. Such a dear boy." The duke opened his mouth to say he had, indeed, met Andrew, but was not given the opportunity. Mrs. Long rushed on. "And such a nice change for Mama, too, don't you know. There is absolutely no one in the country, especially this time of year when everyone comes to London, don't you know. And that is especially true for our little Betsy. She needs young people her own age to frolic with. And it is time she got some town bronze, don't you know. So here we all are. Got here last night, and I daresay it will be just like old times," she finished airily.

The duke, in a state of shock, merely nodded.

His grandmother, too, seemed to be in shock. "I shall ring for tea," she announced.

"Don't bother on my account," said the duke suddenly. "I must be leaving. I have a pressing engagement. Only stopped by to pay my regards." He began to rise.

His grandmother looked meaningfully at him. "I am sure it can wait," she said, then mouthed, "Orphans."

Littlefield reluctantly took his seat again. He looked longingly at the door. That was when Miss Elizabeth Brightham, herself, made her appearance.

Well, he thought, at least she wasn't pockmarked. And she didn't appear to have a squint. But she was no beauty. Her nose was a little too short and her mouth a little too full. She did have lovely golden curls and large blue eyes, but her skin was cursed with a dusting of freckles—all across that less-than-perfect nose. Well, she does have a nice figure, admitted Littlefield, running an expert eye over her curves. That should count for something.

But not much. To overcome the social obstacle of such a family, the girl would have to be a diamond of the first water. And that she clearly was not. Let Grandmother disinherit him. He would rather hang out for a rich heiress—no, he would rather starve in the street than lend the consequence of his name to such a family as this.

The girl, a vision of semiloveliness in her pink sprigged muslin gown, tripped daintily into the room, spreading a glowing smile over the general company. Her eyes finally rested on the duke, and it seemed to him they reflected some secret mirth.

"Ah," said her proud grandmama. "Here is our dear little Betsy now, the belle of the London season. Have you ever seen a more lovely girl?"

Yes, thought the duke irritably as the young lady made her curtsy. He rose and bowed over Miss Brightham's hand.

"Lionel, fetch me my shawl from that

chair, please," commanded his grandmother.

Littlefield obeyed, determined now he
was standing to make his excuses and keep
on going right through the drawing-room
door.

"Thank you, dear boy," she murmered
as he draped it over her shoulders. Before
he could leave, she reached up and
grabbed his hand and beckoned him to
bend his head. "If you leave, I vow I shall
send for my solicitors first thing in the
morning," she whispered into his ear.

The duke straightened, his mouth com-
pressed into an angry line, his body stiff
and unbending. He smiled coldly across
the room at Miss Elizabeth Brightham, the
source of his troubles.

She smiled sweetly back at him with an
unspoken invitation to take a seat next to
her on the sofa. The little toad eater! He'd
help her and her wretched family. He'd
find her a match such as she deserved, by
Jove!

The smile on the duke's face warmed
considerably as his brain caught this passing thought. Yes. That was it! He'd help
the wench. So she wished to marry into
the ton, did she? Well, he was sure he
could find someone suitable for a little
climber such as Miss Birdbrain. He sat

next to her on the sofa. "How did you enjoy your trip to London?" he asked.

"I must admit, it was rather exhausting," she replied. "We came by Mail."

Naturally, thought Littlefield, but nodded encouragingly.

"It was quite shocking the way we were squeezed in," said Mrs. Long. "Of course, the mail will only carry four passengers inside. But I found it ridiculously cramped, nonetheless."

"I would rather be inside than on the roof of a coach," said the girl. "That seems rather dangerous." She turned to Littlefield. "Does it not seem dangerous to you, Your Grace?"

Littlefield shrugged. "It can be," he said. "But it can be a great lark, as well."

The girl's eyes widened. "Do you like danger, then?"

What did she think him anyway, a coward? "I am not afraid of danger," said Littlefield.

She sat for a moment, digesting this. "Oh," she said at last. She smiled at the duke. The chit did have a nice smile, he admitted; sunny, so full of . . . what? If he didn't know better, he'd swear it was mischief. But mischievous smiles should be reserved for great ladies bent on dalliance, not for little nobodies from nowhere. "I think you are not at all what I imagined you to be," she informed him.

"And what had you imagined me to be?" he asked, surprised by this remark.

"I thought you would be like a duke I saw once in Bath, at the Lower Assembly Rooms. He was very high in the instep and looked at everyone like this." She pulled down the corner of her mouth and held up an imaginary quizzing glass. Littlefield smiled in spite of her impertinence, and she joined him. "Can you imagine anyone making himself look so ridiculous, all to make others feel small?"

The duke, who had done just such a thing only last season, said, no, he could not imagine such a thing.

"But anyone can see you are not conceited and hard-hearted like that. Why, anyone with eyes in their head can see that you are a kind-hearted man. Else why would you insist we come stay with your grandmama?"

Littlefield looked at the girl suspiciously. Was she toad-eating him? Was she mocking him? Or, worse yet, had his grandmother told her such a thing? She sat smiling at him, head cocked like some odd little bird. "I am afraid I must disabuse you of a mistaken notion," he said stiffly.

"It was entirely my grandmother's idea for you to come stay with her."

"I see," she said slowly, and her smile grew.

Littlefield was suddenly sure she did, indeed, see, and found himself, for some odd reason, blushing. This, he decided, was not a woman with whom one could be comfortable. In fact, this was a curst impertinent female who deserved to be taught a lesson. And who better to teach her than the Duke of Littlefield?

Two

That evening His Grace attended a main at the Royal Cockpit in Birdcage Walk, and amongst the crowd of enthusiasts spotted his friend Lord Amhearst.

"Littlefield, you old cur!" Amhearst saluted him fondly. "I've got my blunt riding on the White Pile. Look at the sharp heel on the fellow."

"Mmm," grunted Littlefield.

"Did you meet the new toast of the ton today?" teased his friend, still watching the fighting cocks.

"She is nothing to raise your glass to, I assure you," said Littlefield.

Amhearst nodded sympathetically. "Terrifying, eh?"

"Well, not completely so," admitted the duke fairly. "But hardly a diamond of the first water, which is what she would need to be with no connections."

"Ah, but she has connections," teased Lord Amhearst.

Littlefield frowned. "Yes, and don't she know it."

"A toad eater?" Littlefield made a noise of disgust, and Amhearst looked at him with sympathy. "A pity you cannot tell the old harridan to take the girl and go to Jericho."

"Oh, no. I intend to help my grandmother find the chit a fitting husband," said Littlefield lightly, a wicked glint in his eye.

His friend caught it and said, "Ho, now. What's toward?"

Littlefield shrugged. "If the girl wants a fine husband, she should get a fine husband. Don't you think?"

Amhearst's eyes narrowed. "What scheme are you hatching, you dog?"

The duke surveyed the room. "Who here would make a likely groom for a toad-eating little climber?"

Lord Amhearst grinned and scanned the crowd. "How about Mallory?" he suggested, nodding to a scrawny young man.

Littlefield shook his head. "Too slippery by far. Every female from here to Shropshire has dropped her handkerchief for him. And besides, he has a sizable fortune. I don't want to reward the chit."

Amhearst raised an eyebrow. "I wouldn't call Mallory's blunt a reward, old fellow.

From what his mistress has let drop, it would be more a compensation."

The duke grinned but shook his head. "We can do better," he said.

His friend shrugged and returned his attention to the battling birds.

"Well, well," said Littlefield as his eyes fell on a likely candidate for a suitor for the girl.

Lord Amhearst was distracted from the fight and followed his friend's gaze. "Oh, yes," he chuckled. "Good old Bacon. He's enough to make any bride blush, the fat old toad."

"A toad for a toad eater," quipped Littlefield.

"He ain't got a feather to fly with," observed Amhearst.

"Neither does your bird," observed Littlefield, and left his friend frowning as the cock he had his money on fell dead.

Littlefield crossed the room and hailed a pudgy man in a puce-colored coat. "Bacon, old fellow! How goes it?"

Sir Harry Bacon tried to negotiate his heavy jowls around his shirt points and smiled at the duke. "It goes miserably," he replied. "Got to get leg-shackled this season. M' mother is pressing. Produce an heir and all that. Need blunt, too."

Littlefield nodded understandingly.

Sir Harry shook his head. "Got to tell you, Littlefield, I don't fancy getting tied, having some whey-faced little ninny under foot, always wanting me to take her to balls and asking for pin money. Those Almack's milk and water misses bore me to tears."

"A pity one cannot marry one's mistress," joked Littlefield.

Sir Harry looked shocked. "Good Lord, man. Never jest about such things. She'd bleed me dry within a year! Besides, m' mother would kick up too much dust."

Littlefield laughed at this. "Well, if you've a fancy for something out of the ordinary, my grandmother's sponsoring a chit this season who's an original."

"A bluestocking?" asked Sir Harry suspiciously.

"Good Lord, no," replied Littlefield, irritated. "D' you think I'd foist such a thing on a friend?"

"Come to think on it, no," admitted Sir Harry. "But there must be something the matter with her. Why don't you want her?"

"Me! I have a rich grandmother."

"True, true," admitted Sir Harry. "Lucky fellow."

Littlefield thought of the dance on which his grandmother was leading him. "Yes," he said unenthusiastically. "But I tell you, if I were looking, this girl might interest me. Rather out of the ordinary. Not a diamond of the first water, you understand, but not hard to look at. And interesting. She wouldn't bore you. At least, not in the first year."

Sir Harry Bacon looked suspiciously at Littlefield. "You say she has blunt?"

Most likely not, thought Littlefield. He hedged. "You know my grandmother and all her cit friends."

"Hmmm," said Bacon rubbing the uppermost layer of chin. "And you say she ain't hard on the eyes?"

"If you like, I'll invite you to her come-out ball," offered Littlefield. "Then you can see for yourself."

Bacon clapped him on the back with a pudgy paw. "I must admit you've piqued my interest, old fellow. Damned if I won't let you. What's the chit's name, anyway?"

"Birdham, or something like that," said the duke airily. "Good family."

When the Duke of Littlefield left Sir Harry, he wore a smile nearly as mischievous as Miss Brightham's. A little climbing nobody and a fat dandy. A perfect match!

After a late and roisterous night, the duke was in no mood for a morning summons from his maternal grandmother. He examined himself in his looking glass. Bloodshot eyes and dark circles did not become him. He frowned. His head hurt, and he had no desire to talk with the old girl about the Birdham and her abominable family.

The comforting thought came to him that he could at least honestly tell his grandmother that he was already looking to find a suitable husband for the girl. Ha, ha! Suitable was right. Bacon was a glutton and a fool. He and the Birdham should deal famously together.

As the duke had expected, it was to be a private interview. He was shown into the study at his grandmother's townhouse where she awaited him, nervously drumming her fingers on the desk at which she sat.

"Well, go on and say it," she snapped as the door shut behind him.

"Say what?"

"Tell me how monstrous her family is and what a fool I was to make this offer."

It wouldn't be sporting to gloat. Littlefield shrugged. "The girl is tolerably nice-looking. She should be able to snag someone. As long as you keep the rest of her family hidden away."

"That will not be easy to do, I can tell

you," said Mrs. Whitworth. "For here they all are, descended on me, although the invitation was issued only for Betsy." Mrs. Whitworth shuddered. "I vow Maisy was not so vulgar when I knew her at the seminary. How such a sweet girl can have turned into such a forward creature I have no idea."

The duke found himself trying to imagine his grandmother as a young girl. Was she ever an innocent, trusting little thing such as he met at come-out balls? And if she was, would she have been able to recognize a vulgar, pushy woman in the making? It was an interesting thought, but not one on which he had time to dwell.

"What are we to do?" moaned Mrs. Whitworth.

"We?" countered Littlefield. "It was you who invited them."

"Her," corrected Mrs. Whitworth. "I only offered to take Betsy."

The duke dropped into a chair and stretched his long legs out before him. "We shall, I imagine, proceed as you have planned—procure them vouchers to Almack's and have a come-out ball. I am sure all the ton will want to meet your interesting friend."

His grandmother scowled at him. "I

shall thank you not to be impertinent, young man. I am being serious."

"So am I," said Littlefield. "You cannot send them back. You promised the young lady a season." And besides, he thought, that would end the game—just when I am becoming engrossed.

Mrs. Whitworth fidgeted. "I shall go mad. That child is a terror. And Maisy's mother! She fingers everything. And . . ." Mrs. Whitworth lowered her voice. "Johnston has informed me we are missing a spoon."

The corners of the duke's mouth twitched.

"It is not funny, Lionel!"

"I am sorry," he said, trying to look penitent. "But what's to do? You gave your word. You are trapped."

"I think you are glad of it, you wretched boy," she accused.

"Now, Grandmother," he said. "How can you say such a thing? You know I was against such a scheme from the start."

"Which is exactly why you are enjoying this present situation. You are taking a perverse delight in my discomfort."

"Never, love," he said. He rose and planted a kiss on the top of her head. "We shall come about. Never fear."

She patted the hand resting on her shoulder. "You are a good boy," she said. "And to show you how very good I am,

I shall take Miss Birdham for a drive in Hyde Park this afternoon," he promised.

"Brightham," corrected his grandmother. "That is sweet of you, Lionel. But I warn you, she appears to have hardly a decent gown to her name. Heaven knows what odd thing she may choose to wear."

The duke raised an eyebrow at this. "I hope you mean to spring for some new togs. She'll never take elsewhere."

"Of course I do," snapped Mrs. Whitworth. "We are going shopping first thing tomorrow."

The duke nodded his approval and promised to return at half past four to collect Miss Brideham.

"Brightham," corrected his grandmother irritably.

"Yes, Brighthand," agreed the duke.

At exactly thirty minutes past four, the Duke of Littlefield was ushered into his grandmother's house. Outside, his tiger walked the two high-spirited matched grays that pulled his bright yellow curricle. "Please inform Miss Brighthand that I am here," he told the butler.

Miss Brightham was duly informed, and the duke was kept waiting a good fifteen minutes. When she finally did make her appearance, she didn't look at all worth the wait. She appeared in a faded yellow gown and a bonnet with all manner of flowers and fruits on it. The duke scowled at the offending bonnet.

Miss Brightham could see he was displeased. "You do not care for my bonnet?"

"It looks like a fruit cart," replied Littlefield.

Betsy looked hurt. "I trimmed it myself," she said.

Littlefield reached up and plucked off a wilted-looking cloth rose and a clump of cherries.

"Oh," she gasped. "My bonnet!"

"Is now considerably improved," said Littlefield. "Shall we go?"

She looked at him wide-eyed but said nothing, preceding him out the door. Her misery over her desecrated bonnet was short-lived. "Oh, my!" she cried, catching sight of the duke's curricle. "Such a fine-looking carriage."

"It is a curricle," the duke corrected her.

"Oh, no," she said. "It is a magic carpet." She picked up her skirt and ran down the front walk.

He smiled and strolled after her. It was a fine equipage. At least the girl had discriminating taste in something.

Once up on the seat, Miss Brightham sat surveying the world below her. "I have never sat in a curricle," she said. "This is so high, like sitting on top of the world."

"A little," agreed the duke pleasantly. He cracked his whip, and the horses took off at a trot.

Miss Brightham sat beside him in silence, looking about, admiring the elegant houses lining the street. Oddly refreshing to find a lady who didn't jabber at one constantly and expect one to make clever conversation, thought Littlefield.

Ten minutes passed without a word from Miss Brightham. Was she incapable of carrying on a conversation? The duke stole a look at her.

As if feeling his gaze upon her, she turned her head and smiled at him—that same sunny, mischievous smile. "I suppose I should say something witty and entertaining to you. It is the least I can do since you have been kind enough to take me driving. But, truth to tell, I haven't the least notion what to say to amuse a duke," she confessed.

"Tell me about your life," suggested Littlefield.

"Oh, that would surely not entertain you," she said, shaking her head. "Shall I tell you, instead, what I would like my life to be?"

"If you wish," said Littlefield.

"I should like to travel the world—be a lady explorer."

"Ladies don't explore," pointed out His Grace.

She sighed. "I know. And I think it a great pity. Why should one be punished for being a female? Men are allowed to do all sorts of interesting things. They go to war and fight duels. They go away to school and travel. Ladies only stay at home and work needlepoint."

"When they marry, ladies often travel with their husbands," said Littlefield.

Miss Brightham conceded this point with a nod. "It is something to be said for marrying."

"You do not sound as if you think highly of the state of matrimony.

"Oh, I don't know what I think of it, actually," she said. "I suppose matrimony is not so bad if one's husband is tolerable. Of course, my poor mama's husband was very bad, which is why matrimony was not pleasant for her, but Grandmama assures me that I need not fare as my mother did."

Now the duke's interest was piqued. "And how did she fare?"

"Very poorly, indeed. My father was a wastrel. That's what Grandmama says.

They were all very deceived in him. He left Mama when I was quite small."

Littlefield's eyes widened. Here was shocking news, indeed! What sort of havey-cavey family was this?

"Grandmama said no one was sorry when he was killed," continued Miss Brightham matter-of-factly.

The duke dropped the reins and the horses frolicked. "What?" he demanded.

"My father. He was killed. I believe he was killed in some gambling establishment. However, I am not sure, for neither Mama nor Grandmama cared to speak of it."

"Thank heaven there is something the old woman don't talk about," muttered the duke.

"I beg your pardon?" asked Miss Brightham.

"Nothing, nothing," he said, then fell into thoughtful silence. A gaming hell, eh? Littlefield knew them well enough. He had haunted his share in his younger years. Nearly been killed once in such a place, himself. Little Miss Brightham's father had been a wild one, no doubt about it. Poor girl.

"Of course, we have rubbed along very well," she continued. "My father did leave a little money behind—enough to keep us in a sweet little cottage and enough,

Grandmama says, for me to have a dowry.
It wasn't long after when Mama met the
vicar—my papa now—who adopted me, and
then Andrew was born, and we have all
been most comfortable ever since." She
brightened. "So I suppose matrimony
worked out quite well for Mama in the
end, did it not?"

"Er, yes," agreed the duke. This was the
chit's idea of a good match, marriage to
a vicar?

"Is anything wrong?" asked Miss Brightham.

"Er, no." The duke fell into a state of
silent cogitation. "Perhaps," he said after
a while, "it would be best not to mention
anything to anyone about your father."

"The vicar?"

"No. Your first father."

Miss Brightham blushed. "Oh. It would
not be proper?" she guessed.

"Most likely not," said the duke gently.
"At least not the part about him running
off and leaving you."

Miss Brightham bit her lip. "I suppose
it was not proper to tell you," she ventured. "But you are almost like my guardian, being Mrs. Whitworth's grandson and
all, so surely you should know," she added.

Guardian! Guardians were old and
stodgy. How old did she think him, any-

way? "Well, I wouldn't exactly call me a guardian," he began. How the devil did getting vouchers and lending his house for a ball make him a guardian? He didn't want to be responsible for the chit!

"A guardian angel," she amended. "A big handsome guardian angel. Angels are all men," she informed him. "The vicar told me so."

Littlefield laughed at this and shook his head. "I am no angel," he said.

Miss Brightham smiled her mischievous smile at this. "I'll wager you aren't," she agreed. She sighed. "What a pity Mama is not alive to enjoy our big adventure. I imagine she would be a great help in showing me how to go on."

Once again, the duke found himself taken by surprise. The mother was dead? Of course! That would explain the presence of the grandmother. She had settled her daughter, not once but twice. And now, years later, as determined for her granddaughter, she had invoked the help of a well-connected old acquaintance to make sure the girl was properly launched. He had to hand it to the old woman. She'd used her wits.

The rest of the drive passed pleasantly, more pleasantly than the duke could have imagined, in fact. And as they pulled up in front of his grandmother's townhouse, he found himself feeling oddly sad to see their time together come to an end. 'Tis a pleasant game I'm playing, he told himself, sizing up Miss Brightham and seeing how I can pass her off as quality. I simply hate to end the game so early today. That is all I am feeling. Nothing more.

He handed her down from the curricle. She had small, dainty hands, he noticed. "I hope you enjoyed our drive, Miss Brightham," he said politely.

"Don't you think if you are going to be my guardian angel you should call me by my first name?" suggested Miss Brightham.

"It is hardly proper for me to be calling a young lady I have just met by her first name," said Littlefield, and was disgusted with himself. He sounded so stodgy, so proper. Was this the same man who only a week before had delighted in making improper advances to a nervous young lady in the Dark Walk at Vauxhall Gardens?

"Guardian angels never call people by their surnames," said Miss Brightham. "Besides, it would make me feel ever so much less nervous about everything that lies ahead of me if you did. Rather like having an older brother, don't you know?"

An older brother? Was that how she saw

him? Harmless? Well, and what did he
care how the chit saw him? "Oh, very
well," he said, sounding more petulant
than gracious. "What shall I call you?"

"Betsy, if you please."

The duke cringed. "How would it be if
I were to call you Elizabeth?" he suggested.

The young lady wrinkled her nose. "I
have always been Betsy."

"You have always been a little girl. Until
now," pointed out the duke. "If you are
to make your way in London society, you
had best become Elizabeth."

She considered this. "Very well. Elizabeth. And I shall call you . . ."

"Your Grace," supplied Littlefield
dampingly.

"Only when we are in public," she said.
"In private I shall call you Gabriel."

"Gabriel! That's a curst silly name," protested Littlefield.

"No, it's not!" declared Betsy. "It is the
name of a very important guardian angel.
And I like it."

"Well, I don't, and I'll thank you not to
call me such a silly thing," he said firmly.

She gave in. "Very well," she said
meekly. And added, "Your Grace," in a
teasing tone.

The duke opened his mouth to scold
her for her impertinence, but they had

reached the door of his grandmother's townhouse and the butler was opening it, so he settled for giving her a stern look.

She lowered her eyes demurely under his gaze, but she didn't seem at all chastened, not with those dimples appearing on either side of her mouth. The vixen!

Well, we'll see how often those dimples show when I start putting you through your paces, my girl, he thought.

"I suppose I shan't see you tomorrow," she said, and not at all regretfully. "I am sure we shall be much too busy shopping."

"I hate to disabuse you of your notions, but I intend to come with you," said the duke haughtily. "You'll need a man's opinion," he informed her, then took his leave, feeling he had showed Miss Betsy Brightham who was in charge.

Three

The following day the duke arrived at Mrs. Whitworth's house to find things in an uproar. He was shown into the drawing room, where he found his grandmother, Betsy, and Mrs. Long, as well as Andrew. Mrs. Long was alternately scolding little Andrew and pleading with him to be a good boy and not tease the housemaids further.

Andrew, not wishing to hear any more about the matter, was attempting to squeeze past Mrs. Whitworth and out the door, and in doing so, was in the process of upsetting a small table.

The announcement of the Duke of Littlefield's presence put a stop to all action, except the table, which fell and spilled its knicknacks with a noisy crash.

"Here, now," said Littlefield. "What's this?" He strode into the room, and Andrew quailed.

"Andrew is being beastly," accused Betsy.

"I am not," insisted Andrew. "I was only trying to have some fun."

"And just what sort of fun were you trying to have?" asked the duke.

"He was hiding under the beds and grabbing the maids' ankles when they went to make them," accused Betsy angrily. "Scaring them half to death. A very fine way to behave. I am sure Papa will be very proud of you."

The duke knelt down beside the child. "So you were being the monster under the bed, eh?"

Andrew rubbed the Aubusson carpet with the toe of his shoe. "I was just trying to have some fun," he said in a small voice. "And I'm sorry I knocked the table over," he added. His lower lip began to quiver. "I want to go shopping, too."

"So that is what is at the bottom of this," said Mrs. Long. "Now, Andrew. We have been all over this before. You may not go this time."

"I don't see why not," muttered Andrew.

The duke shook his head. "Boring business, shopping. Ladies take forever. They must look at this ell of cloth, then that ell of cloth, then this ell again. 'I don't know, Marguerite. Which color do you like best?' " he asked in a high falsetto, holding an imaginery piece of cloth to his chest. " 'Oh, not that one,' " he replied, now another woman. " 'I much prefer the one we looked at an hour ago.' " Andrew laughed in spite of himself, and Littlefield continued, "Why, a fellow's feet can go to sleep waiting for them. Then they must go look at bonnets. And gloves." Littlefield made a face. "You are most fortunate. You may stay at home. You don't have to stand about and have your feet fall asleep."

"But I don't want to stay home all by myself with nothing to do," said Andrew.

"You behave yourself today and tomorrow I shall take you to see the Tower of London," promised Littlefield. "And to Gunther's for an ice."

Andrew's eyes grew big. "Promise?"

"Of course. Did I not just say I would?"

"Smashing!" cried Andrew, and prepared to dash off.

A large hand caught him by the back of the shirt. "But you had best keep your end of the bargain and behave like a proper gentleman," warned the duke. "For if you don't, I shall grind your bones to make my bread."

Again, Andrew's eyes grew wide. "I will," he squeaked and hurried off.

"My, but that was most amazing," said Mrs. Long. "And how very kind of you to make such an offer, Your Grace. Betsy, dearest, perhaps you would care to accompany the duke and help him take care of Andrew?''

Betsy blushed at such obvious maneuvering. "I think, perhaps, it would be nice for the men to have some time away from the ladies," she said.

"Nonsense," said her grandmama. "The duke has no desire to be stuck with the care of a little boy all day. You may go along and help keep an eye on Andrew. I shall give Nancy the day off."

Littlefield politely insisted Miss Brightham accompany Andrew and him, and the matter was settled. Why not? he thought. If I am to be saddled with the boy, I may as well be saddled with the girl as well. Besides, she entertains me.

The crisis past, the ladies and their escort made their way to Oxford Street to give business to any number of shops. True to his word, Littlefield was very free in giving his opinion on everything from colors for Miss Brightham's gowns to what bonnets became her best. And Mrs. Long received his opinions as if they had been delivered on stone tablets. Whatever the duke pronounced unsuitable was rejected, even if her granddaughter liked it. One bonnet in particular Betsy had wanted desperately, but Littlefield found its outrageous purple plumes offended his sensibilities greatly. She even went so far as to whisper that she would pay him five pounds to change his opinion on it. "Never," he said. "And besides, what would you wear it with?"

"That lilac walking gown we are having made," said Betsy.

"Lord," muttered the duke.

"I think it would look quite charming," she said. "And besides," she finished in a small voice. "I should so like something in my wardrobe which I myself picked out."

"Nonsense," said her grandmother, who had overheard most of the conversation. "If the duke finds it offensive, it cannot be in good taste. And you would certainly not wish to make your social debut and be thought to have no taste." She gave Littlefield a simpering smile. "Is that not so, my dear Duke?"

Littlefield nodded stiffly. Let us hope, he thought snidely, that as family is not a matter of choice, no one will think Miss Brightham's a reflection on her taste.

At last the shopping ordeal ended when Mrs. Whitworth declared herself quite exhausted and her feet sore beyond bearing.

"Oh, dear. Poor Jane," said Mrs. Long. "You were never very strong."

"I was perfectly strong," declared Mrs. Whitworth. "And there is still nothing wrong with my constitution. But a day such as we have had would cause even an ox to collapse."

"How true," said her old friend. "And you have done so much for us, dearest. So very kind. And to think that clever young woman will have Betsy's gowns done so quickly. Of course, I am sure that is because of our important companion, don't you know," she said, beaming on the duke. She turned again to Mrs. Whitworth. "I know the vicar will wish to reimburse you."

Everyone present knew the vicar's entire yearly stipend couldn't pay for the wardrobe that had been purchased that day. "Think nothing of it," said Mrs. Whitworth graciously. "I am, naturally, happy to help." Her grandson smiled teasingly at her, but she chose not to see.

The following morning the duke presented himself once more at the Whitworth townhouse and found Andrew behind the butler, hopping excitedly from foot to foot. "I am ready," he announced.

"And so am I," said Littlefield. "Where is your sister?"

"She does not go," announced Andrew. "She has the headache. Grandmama scolded her something horrible, but she said she would not go."

At that moment, Grandmama herself descended the stairs. "Oh, Your Grace," she cried. "I am afraid my poor child is most unwell. All yesterday's excitement must have been too much for her. Of course, we shall have to postpone the outing."

"But, Grandmama," protested Andrew. "The duke promised."

"Andrew. You cannot expect the poor duke to go traipsing about the Tower of London with you all by himself," said his grandmother quellingly.

"Of course he can," said Littlefield. "A promise is a promise. Come along, then," he said to Andrew. "My curricle is outside, and I don't wish to keep my horses standing any longer."

With a shout of glee, the little boy ran out the door before him.

"Oh, my. Are you sure? Such a dear boy. So very good of you," gushed Mrs. Long. "I don't know how we shall ever be able to—"

"No need," Littlefield cut her off and sauntered out after the child. Such a woman! He sincerely hoped his grandmother Hopewell did not encounter her until after Elizabeth's voucher for Almack's was secured, else the game would surely be up.

Andrew thoroughly enjoyed the Tower of London. So did the duke, once he made it clear to the child that he did not intend to chase him from courtyard to corridor, and that Andrew had best keep beside him. Andrew was not at first happy at the prospect of slowing his steps to match a grownup's, but after a stern look from Littlefield, he complied and found he could enjoy the Tower almost as much at a slower pace. He especially enjoyed the grizzly site where Queen Anne Boleyn lost her head over Henry VIII. And he was very impressed with the Beefeaters in their puffy red uniforms. "Why are they called Beefeaters?" he asked.

"How the devil should I know?" countered Littlefield.

"You are a duke," said the boy simply.

"Well, even dukes don't know everything," said Littlefield.

Their visit to the Tower was such a success, and the duke was feeling so pleased with himself, that he took the boy along to Haymarket, where they visited Week's Mechanical Museum. Andrew's eyes grew wide and bright at the sight of the musical clocks and mechanical birds and mice and other animals the establishment displayed.

"When I grow up, I shall make a musical clock and give it to Betsy," he announced.

"I am sure she will like that," said Littlefield soberly. He studied the boy. "Do you like your sister so very much, then?"

"Oh, yes," said Andrew. "Most of the time she is very much fun. She plays hide-and-go-seek and Puss in the Corner with me and tells me stories. Sometimes she scolds me or tells me to go away and not bother her, but most of the time she doesn't," he finished fairly. "Papa plays spillikins with us sometimes," he offered after a while.

Here was an interesting piece of information. Somehow, the duke found it hard to imagine a vicar doing such a thing. Vicars weren't supposed to have fun, were they?

"Are we still going to go have an ice?" asked Andrew.

"A promise is a promise," said Littlefield.

At Gunther's, they stuffed themselves on ices and biscuits, and, at the duke's suggestion, carried home some sugar plums to poor Betsy, who had missed out on all the fun, as Andrew put it.

Yes, thought Littlefield. She *had* missed out on the fun. Had she kept away purposely to tease him? He put aside this idea as soon as it came. Ridiculous. What woman in her right mind would refuse such an opportunity?

A vision of Miss Brightham, blushing and protesting after her grandmama's overt maneuvering to throw her together with him came to mind. Perhaps she didn't wish to appear forward. Was she playing the coquette? Trying to pique his interest? Ha! That was most amusing. A little nobody trying to lead the Duke of Littlefield around by the nose. He wished her luck in that.

"I had a very good time," said Andrew as they left the shop. He put his hand in Littlefield's and smiled up at him. "Did you?"

His Grace had to admit that he did.

Andrew was returned to his grandmama, along with the sugar plums for his sister. The duke refused all offers of refreshment—tea, sherry, a biscuit—pleading another engagement, and left one grandmother's house for the other's.

He was fortunate to find the duchess at home, and was shown up to her sitting room. "Lionel. Where have you been, dear boy?"

She gave him her cheek to kiss. He complied and seated himself in a dainty Hepplewhite chair. "I have been busy getting

acquainted with Grandmother Whitworth's
protégée."

Her Grace frowned. "Oh, yes. I had almost forgotten."

"I feared you might," said Littlefield.
"Which is why I am here."

"Well, and how do you find the child?"

"Amusing," answered Littlefield, brushing a speck from his coat sleeve. "She will
enliven the season greatly, and I would be
obliged if you would use your influence in
obtaining a voucher for her."

"Amusing," snorted Her Grace. "That
tells me little enough. What is her family?"

"Merely respectable. A vicar. Most likely,
a second son."

"A vicar! Most likely a third or fourth
son," said Her Grace scornfully. "Lionel,
you must be mad." She studied her grandson. "It is the money, isn't it?" she accused. "That woman holds it over your
head."

"She does," admitted Littlefield. "But I
can assure you it is not my primary reason
for wishing Miss Brightham well." He
smiled wickedly. "I have every intention of
helping her achieve a suitable match."

"What! You would help this little climber
make a brilliant match?"

"I would help this little climber make a

match suitable for a climber," said Little-field.

His grandmother studied him and at last caught his meaning. She began to chuckle. "Oh, very well. I shall let you have your fun," she said. "I shall send for Lady Jersey. The girl owes me a favor. Perhaps I can convince her to risk a voucher on this young lady." Littlefield beamed, and the duchess held up a staying hand. "However, I make no promises. I have little influence with any of those women, and favor or no, Lady Jersey may deny me. The most Mrs. Whitworth can hope for is a visit."

The duke left his grandmother's presence, well-pleased. Lady Jersey was the head of the committee of patronesses of Almack's, bastion of elitism. Her support would ensure the Birdham's success. The girl was nice enough. It shouldn't be too difficult for her to secure her ladyship's approval and gain an entrance to that establishment and the very select society that patronized it. Then everyone would be happy. His grandmother would be pleased with him for helping her fulfill a promise to a tiresome girlhood friend; the intriguing little climber would be happy to have her social success ensured; he would remain in his grandmother's will and have a most entertaining season to boot.

Miss Elizabeth Brightham's future having been so easily taken care of, the duke went off to his townhouse, where he changed his clothes. Then he went on to Brooks's at Number Sixty in St. James's, in search of male companionship, the memory of Miss Brightham's mischievous smile trailing him all the way like a stray puppy.

Two days after his visit to the dowager duchess, the duke received an anxious summons from Mrs. Whitworth. "What now?" he muttered, crumpling the offending stationery and tossing it on the fire.

As requested, he presented himself at his grandmother's study at twelve o'clock, having first had to shake an enthusiastic Mrs. Long, who hoped the dear duke intended to remain and take a dish of tea. The thought of tea at any time was less than exciting to Littlefield. At twelve o'clock in the morning it was enough to make him bilious. He informed Mrs. Long that his call was purely business and wished her good day, shutting the door firmly in her face.

His grandmother greeted him with a

shaking head and rolling eyes. "You see what my life is like," she said in tragic accents. "And pray, don't say it is as much as I deserve, for I know it. I am missing a piece of Dresden," she added.

"Andrew has broken it, most like," said the duke, unconcerned.

Mrs. Whitworth sighed and shook her head. "Well, that is nothing compared to this fresh trouble which presents itself. And I tell you frankly, Lionel, I know not what to do."

His grandmother Whitworth not knowing what to do? Here was trouble, indeed. "What new tragedy befalls the house of Whitworth?" teased Littlefield.

"Lady Jersey," said Mrs. Whitworth.

"Lady Jersey? I don't understand. Grandmother promised me only two days ago she would speak to her about a voucher for Elizabeth."

"Oh, she has," said Mrs. Whitworth miserably. "Lady Jersey is coming to call this afternoon."

The duke shrugged. "Then she can meet Elizabeth and . . ."

"Her grandmother," supplied Mrs. Whitworth, "and her great-grandmother, and . . ."

"Oh, no," said the duke.

"Precisely," said Mrs. Whitworth.

Four

"Where is Elizabeth now?" asked Littlefield.

"In the drawing room," replied his grandmother.

"I shall see her," he condescended, and headed for the drawing room to inspect Betsy. He found her hard at work beading a reticule.

She smiled at him in greeting. "Your Grace. How kind of you to call."

"Stand up," commanded Littlefield.

Betsy stood, the smile nearly erased from her face.

The duke walked to each side of her, studying all angles. The figure was definitely pleasing. But the gown . . . it would never do. The Duke of Littlefield was no dandy, but he knew enough of fashion to know when a lady was wearing a gown of inferior make. "When do your new gowns arrive?" he asked.

"I have my final fitting tomorrow," said Betsy and gave him a questioning look.

Littlefield frowned. "That will never do," he said. "I shall send a note to the dressmaker that we need a morning gown delivered within the hour," he said.

"Within the hour!" gasped Betsy. "How can she possibly have a gown ready so soon?"

"She is being paid enough," said Littlefield heartlessly.

"Oh, dear," fretted Betsy. "I should hate to have that poor woman distressed on my account. I am sure I can get by until she has had time to finish of her own accord."

"You cannot, as you put it, 'get by' greeting Lady Jersey in a gown like that," observed Littlefield. "Did your grandmother not tell you her ladyship intends to call today?"

"Well, yes, but . . ." Betsy bit her lip and looked down at her dress. "I did not think it such a terrible gown." She looked at the hem. "I did the embroidery myself."

Littlefield suddenly felt the cruelest of monsters. "It is not such a bad gown," he amended. "But you want to put your best foot forward when you meet old Silence."

"Silence? What a very odd name," mused Betsy.

"She has been given that name for a reason," said Littlefield. "I can assure you, Miss Brightham, that if Lady Jersey finds you lacking, the entire ton will soon know it."

"Oh, dear," said Betsy, impressed.

"And I am afraid," continued the duke, "that she will have only to see your gown, which I am sure was most serviceable back at the vicarage but won't do here in London, and find you lacking."

Betsy sighed. "Very well," she said. "I suppose we will have to hope it won't be too much trouble for the dressmaker to finish it."

"Trouble or no, she will finish it," said the duke in the voice of one who knew his orders would be obeyed.

"I only hope it will fit," muttered Betsy.

"If it does not, your maid will have to pin the parts that don't," said Littlefield briskly. He rang the bellpull and Johnston, the butler, appeared. "Send a footman to Madame Burnoose's and inform her that the Duke of Littlefield needs a morning gown finished immediately for Miss Betsy . . ."

"Brightham," provided Betsy helpfully.

"Yes, Brightham," continued the duke. "Inform her it is needed within the hour. He may tell her she will be paid handsomely for this." Here the duke looked at

Betsy as if to say, "There. Are you happy now?" and she smiled at him. He continued, "The footman is to wait and bring the thing home the second it is finished." The butler bowed and left, and Littlefield turned again to Betsy. "Now, let me see you curtsy."

The duke spent the next forty minutes drilling Betsy, barking orders, questioningly her mercilessly. "Really!" she finally exclaimed in exasperation. "It is not as if I had no social graces."

"Do you wish to make a good impression or not?" demanded Littlefield, irritated with her lack of gratitude.

It was at this moment that Mrs. Long entered the room. "Now, what is this I am hearing? I hope you are not having words with our dear duke."

"Our dear duke is treating me as if I were a green girl not yet out of the schoolroom," said Betsy, looking accusingly at Littlefield. "And all because Lady Jersey is coming to call."

"Lady Jersey? Coming here?" Mrs. Long looked like a general receiving news that her camp was about to be overrun with enemy soldiers. "Is she not one of the patronesses?"

Littlefield nodded.

"Oh, my! Betsy, let me see you curtsy."

"I have already curtsyed for the duke. Twenty-two times."

"Then do it a twenty-third," boomed her grandmother.

Betsy curtsied.

"Well, now. I am sure even Lady Jersey can find no fault with that," approved her grandmother. "Oh, dear. I do wish your new gowns were ready. When is her ladyship coming?"

"Today," said Betsy gloomily.

"Today!" squeaked Mrs. Long. "Oh, dear!"

"Don't worry, Grandmama," said Betsy lightly. "The duke's command has already gone out, and even as we speak, Madame Burnoose is working feverishly to complete a morning gown for me."

The scorn in her voice was plain, and the duke, hearing it, frowned.

But Mrs. Long was oblivious. "Thank God," she breathed.

An hour later, Mrs. Whitworth joined them. "I am sure we can expect Lady Jersey at any time," she fretted.

"Oh, not before the gown arrives," prayed Mrs. Long.

As if on cue, the footman appeared, bearing a large box. "Have it carried to Miss Brightham's room," ordered the duke. Then, to Betsy, "Go put it on, then come down immediately and show me."

"Yes, Your Majes—er, Your Grace," said Betsy with a low bow, and hurried out of the room before Littlefield could put her in her place with a proper set-down.

Insolent chit! This was the thanks he received for sacrificing his time to help her.

"Our little Betsy does have such lively spirits," said Mrs. Long nervously.

"She would do well to drain some of the life out of them," said the duke dampingly.

"Oh, yes, Your Grace. You are so right. If you will excuse me, I shall just go and see how the gown fits. Please . . . excuse . . ." Mrs. Long made a hasty curtsy and fled.

Feeling somewhat mollified that someone at least knew what respect was due him, Littlefield plopped onto a wing chair.

"Really, Lionel," scolded his grandmother, "there is no need to bark orders at the child."

The duke raised an eyebrow. "I was hardly barking orders. I am only, in fact, here at your request. If you wish, I could leave."

"If you leave, I shall send for my solicitor," snapped his grandmother, and left him to wonder what he could have done to deserve being visited with such a trial.

He had still to answer the question when Betsy returned, an accusing look on her face. Her grandmother accompanied her, assuring her that, really, the gown did not look so very bad.

The duke took in Miss Brightham's disappointed frown and then the gown. Something was not right. He got from his chair and walked over to Betsy for a closer examination.

"The bodice is too big," she informed him. "I daresay Madame Burnoose could have corrected that if I had been allowed a second fitting."

Littlefield ignored the accusing tone in her voice. "It can be pinned, can it not?"

"Yes, but—" began Betsy.

"Then pin it," he said shortly. "And get that maid of yours to do something with your hair."

"As you wish," she said sweetly, giving him a deep curtsy.

As she did so, the loose bodice gaped, giving Littlefield an equally sweet view of her breasts.

When she rose, it was to see the duke, instead of glowering in perturbation, smiling lecherously at her. She looked at the offending bodice, turned a bright crimson, and pushed the fabric to her chest, giving him a reprimanding look. "If you will excuse me," she said. The duke bowed, and she marched from the room, his laughter echoing after her.

She had barely left when the butler entered the drawing-room door and presented Littlefield with Lady Jersey's calling card.

Littlefield sprang to his feet, feeling suddenly unaccountably nervous. "Bring her up," he said.

Lady Jersey sailed into the room. She stopped in surprise at the sight of the duke. A smile lit her face. "Why, Littlefield. What are you doing here?" The duke bowed over her hand, and she smiled on him. "This young lady must be a diamond of the first water to draw the Duke of Littlefield to her drawing room." She gave him an arch look. "Or is it familial duty?"

At that moment his grandmother entered the room and did obeisance. "Your ladyship. You honor me greatly. Pray, be seated."

"The duchess has told me of your protégée, Mrs. Whitworth. I find myself consumed by curiosity. Is she at home to callers?"

"Oh, yes," said Mrs. Whitworth. "She

will be with us momentarily. May I offer you tea?"

"That would be nice," said Lady Jersey in a condescending voice. "I hope you have had some proper gowns made for the child," she advised. "A young lady can hardly hope to be a success without the proper attire."

"We have," said Mrs. Whitworth.

"And who is your dressmaker?" inquired Lady Jersey.

"Madame Burnoose."

"Not the best," observed her ladyship.

Mrs. Whitworth bristled, and to prevent disaster, Littlefield rushed into the conversation, asking after the health of her ladyship's family.

Her ladyship started with her own state of health and had gotten no further when Betsy finally made her appearance. Her gown fit much better now, Littlefield noticed with satisfaction. The maid had done an excellent job of pinning it; the duke could detect no sign of pins.

Lady Jersey smiled graciously. "Ah, and is this our young lady? Aren't you a sweet-looking thing?"

The duke smiled and hoped Miss Elizabeth Brightbird realized how very much she owed him.

Elizabeth was in the process of making

a very stiff curtsy when Mrs. Long appeared. "Ah, Lady Jersey! Such an honor it is to meet you. Of course, I have heard so much about you, don't you know. My first son-in-law, I believe, knew you. My, my, but you are ever so much more lovely than I imagined."

Lady Jersey's smile showed she was torn between enjoying Mrs. Long's flattery and being insulted by her familiarity. It could go either way, thought the duke, and wondered how he could get Mrs. Long out of the room.

Mrs. Long seated herself next to her ladyship and said, "Well, now, my dear young woman, you must tell me how you came up with the idea for establishing such a gathering place as Almack's. I am sure it was most clever. And such a good idea to keep it exclusive."

"Yes," said Lady Jersey coldly.

Not good, thought Littlefield. That was when Betsy twitched and caught her ladyship's eye.

Betsy blushed and smiled.

The duke, having witnessed this strange interchange, ignored Mrs. Long's rattling and studied Betsy, who was now sitting attentively. What the devil had caused that odd start? Suddenly, he knew. By Jove, this is rich, he thought. The chit is sitting on pins and needles. Literally. He gave a delicate cough, hiding a chuckle, and Betsy flashed an angry look his direction.

The butler arrived with the tea tray. "Perhaps you would care to pour, Betsy dear?" suggested Mrs. Long. "Our Betsy has always been the picture of grace when presiding over the tea tray. You may go," she said grandly to the butler.

Betsy looked highly nervous at this suggestion, but complied. She leaned over to pick up the teapot, jumped, and let out a yelp. "Excuse me," she murmered and tried again, leaning forward very carefully.

The duke noticed that Lady Jersey was looking at Betsy curiously. If you plan to amuse us by spilling tea, he thought, watching Betsy as well, pray don't spill it on Silence.

This time Betsy managed to get the tea poured into the cup. "Sugar?" she asked.

"And a little cream," said her ladyship.

Betsy complied and leaned forward with the cup. Again she jumped and let out a squeak. The cup rattled and tipped in the saucer, spilling the hot liquid, causing Betsy to drop the cup.

"Oh, my dear child! Are you quite alright?" exclaimed Mrs. Long. "Someone ring for the butler," she commanded. She then turned to Lady Jersey and said, "My poor granddaughter hurt her back playing with her little brother the other day. I completely forgot. How thoughtless of me to cause you to strain it," she said to Betsy.

Quick improvising, thought the duke with admiration, and settled back to see what new challenge would arise. This little party was proving quite entertaining.

The butler was dispatched to fetch towels to clean the mess. Shortly after he returned, a new challenge arrived in the form of Mrs. Long's mama.

"Ah, here is Granny," announced Mrs. Long. "Come, sit down, and you shall have some tea. Now, Granny, you just sit here on the other side of Lady Jersey, and we shall all be as comfortable as peas in a pod."

The crone sat and eyed the tea tray. Lady Jersey smiled uncomfortably at the company in general. Her smile changed to a look of shock as the old woman darted out a quick hand, snatched up a spoon, and tucked it beneath her shawl.

Mrs. Whitworth shot her grandson a look of panic, and he gave her a helpless look in return.

Mrs. Long appeared not to have seen and was chattering on about how cozy they all were when a muffled sneeze distracted her. She looked around the room and spied a vertical bulge in the heavy drapes. "Andrew!" she scolded.

A small, curly-topped head poked around the drape. "Hullo Grandmama," said Andrew, giving the assembled company his sweetest smile.

"And who is this?" asked Lady Jersey, obviously charmed.

"This is my naughty grandson," said Mrs. Long."

"I only wanted to see the great lady," said Andrew contritely.

"Well, come here, young man, and so you shall," said her ladyship.

Andrew obeyed.

"Your name is Andrew, is it?"

Andrew nodded.

"That is a fine name," said her ladyship.

"Thank you," said Andrew politely.

Littlefield smiled. The boy was a real piece of luck.

Andrew cocked his head and regarded Lady Jersey. "You do have a great deal of hair, don't you?" he said at last.

She smiled tolerantly. "Why, yes. I believe I do."

Andrew nodded as if this answered something. "Mrs. Whitworth said you have more hair than wit."

Mrs. Whitworth choked on her tea, and Mrs. Long gasped. The smile fell from

Lady Jersey's face, and she drew herself
up as if for battle.

"Andrew!" cried Mrs. Long. "I am sure
Mrs. Whitworth said no such thing. What
a wicked thing to say!"

"But she did, Grandmama. Is it wicked?
I did not know."

"I am afraid I must be going," said
Lady Jersey coldly, setting aside her teacup.

"Oh, but surely there is no need to go
rushing off," protested Mrs. Long ur-
gently. "One should pay no attention to
children. They are always mixing up what
they have heard."

"I am sure that is true in most in-
stances," agreed her ladyship coldly. "I bid
you good day."

As soon as Lady Jersey had made her
grand exit, Mrs. Long turned on the quiv-
ering Andrew. "Now, young man," she
said, taking him by the ear and leading
him away, "see the trouble you have
caused!" Andrew howled and Mrs. Long
raised her voice and continued, "You may
march straight off to your bedroom and
remain there and think about the fine
supper you shall miss, which is no less
than naughty boys who spy and tattle deserve!" She let loose of his ear and gave
him a whack on the bottom, and, still cry-
ing gustily, he ran off. With slumping

shoulders, she then rejoined the rest of the company in the drawing room.

A glum silence fell over them. All except Granny, who was humming softly to herself and playing with the fringe on her shawl.

Betsy sighed. "Poor Andrew."

"Poor Andrew!" echoed Mrs. Long. "He is the cause of all our troubles! It is due to his naughtiness that we have lost all hope of getting vouchers for Almacks."

"Oh, Grandmama," sighed Betsy. "I am sure I lost our vouchers the moment I dropped the teacup."

Mrs. Long sighed as well. "Perhaps she will reconsider."

"When pigs fly," muttered Littlefield, and wondered why he felt so sour. After all, the visit had been an amazing spectacle, and the recounting of it would amuse old Amhearst heartily.

But here was the girl, looking as if her best friend had died. Even the hearty nuisance, Mrs. Long, appeared suddenly very old and tired.

"You are just as well off without those vouchers, if you ask me," said Mrs. Whitworth. "A more vain and conceited creature I am sure I never saw. And all the nobility is the same. You would be much better off to find a nice young man who is not all caught up in himself, who values more in life than position and pleasure."

Littlefield bristled at this. "Here now! That is hardly fair," he objected.

"But fairly true," retorted his grandmother. She returned her attention to Betsy, and her face softened. "Now, don't cry, child. Lionel will think of something."

"Me!" choked Littlefield. "I have no influence with those women. Why, even Wellington does their bidding—showed up once at Almacks' in pantaloons and they sent him packing."

"Lionel!" snapped Mrs. Whitworth. Returning her attention to Betsy, she smiled encouragingly. "I am sure things will work out," she said.

Betsy looked at Littlefield with hope in her eyes. "If anyone can do anything, it must be the duke," she said confidently.

The duke said nothing and, as soon as possible, took his leave.

"Grandmama," said Betsy earnestly after he had gone, "perhaps we had best return home. It does not matter so very much to me to be a part of the ton."

"Nonsense," said her grandmother firmly. "You deserve to be and so you shall. I shan't rest until we have succeeded in planting you firmly in society and finding you a suitable husband."

"Yes, Grandmama," said Betsy meekly. She took in a deep breath, got poked by a pin, and let out a yelp. "Oh, my," she said, her voice unsteady. "I think it is high time I got out of this ridiculous gown. Please excuse me."

Mrs. Long watched her go. "Poor lambkin," she said softly. "Ah, Jane. Did you ever meet a sweeter child?"

Mrs. Whitworth had to admit that she had not. She leaned over and patted her friend's arm. "Don't worry. If anyone can help her, it is Littlefield."

"If he is so inclined," said Mrs. Long glumly.

"He will feel so inclined, I assure you," predicted Mrs. Whitworth.

In her room, Betsy breathed a sigh of relief as she stepped out of the gown. She raised her arm to inspect the little scratches on her side and shook her head. "All for naught," she sighed.

A shy knocking at her door announced a visitor. Her abigail helped her into a dressing gown, then opened the door to admit Master Andrew, looking pitifully penitent. His lower lip trembled. "Betsy, I did not mean to make the great lady angry," he began, then burst into tears.

Betsy rushed to kneel in front of the child and take him in her arms. "There now," she murmered. "Everything is going to be fine. Don't you fret."

"Grandmama is very angry with me," hiccoughed Andrew between sobs.

"Yes, she is," agreed Betsy. "But by tomorrow she will have forgotten to be angry. You will see."

"But she will still be angry with me tonight," pointed out Andrew. "And I am already very hungry."

Betsy smiled at this. "Never you fear. I shall smuggle some buns and milk to you. How will that be?"

A sunny smile lighted Andrew's tear-stained face. "Oh, that will be very nice," he said.

"Now," said Betsy, rising. "You had best run along to your room before Grandmama finds you are not there and becomes angry with you all over again."

Andrew's eyes grew wide with appreciative horror, and he scampered off. She watched him go and smiled. "Wouldn't it be wonderful," she said to her abigail, "if all our problems could so easily be solved?"

The duke made his way to Brooks's, and there encountered his friend, Lord Amhearst. "Well, strap me if I wasn't just thinking of you," he greeted Amhearst amiably, falling into a wing chair across from the one where his friend lounged.

Amhearst swung a leg to and fro over the arm of the chair and raised an inquiring eyebrow.

"Where do you think I have been today?" said Littlefield casually.

"To see your tailor? You could use a new coat. I am heartily sick of that one."

Littlefield held out a sleeve and inspected it. "Yes, I suppose I, also, have seen enough of it," he agreed. Thoughtfully, he inspected his waistcoat. Perhaps it was time to get a new waistcoat as well.

"If not to your tailor, where did you go?" asked Amhearst.

Recalled to the subject at hand, the duke grinned. "I have been watching my little climber attempt to take the citadel."

"Lady Jersey?" guessed his lordship. "So, she has made her call of inspection?"

Littlefield nodded. "And such a call it was." He then proceeded with much exaggeration and theatrical flair to describe Lady Jersey's visit. Before he was finished, he had Lord Amhearst, as well as two other friends who had stopped to say hello, pulling out their handkerchiefs and mopping their eyes.

The other two men finally moved on to the subscription room to play cards and spread the amusing tale. Lord Amhearst slouched comfortably in his chair and stretched his long legs out before him and shook his head, marveling. "Oh, to have been a fly on the wall," he said wistfully. "Ah, well. Now you won't be troubled further with the girl. Nothing for her but to pack up and go home. Pity, though. Your scheme promised to be great sport. But we all know that even a duke must bow to a ruler of Almack's."

Littlefield grimaced. "Ridiculous how one woman could so hold the fate of another in her hands."

"But there you have it," said Lord Amhearst callously.

Littlefield tapped his chin. "Almack's has more than one patroness, does it not?"

"There's an entire collection, dear boy," said Amhearst. "Let me see. There is Lady Castlereagh, Princess Esterhazy—she would never let your climber in, I can assure you—Countess Lieven, Lady Cowper, Drummond Burrell—there is a toplofty tabby for you." Lord Amhearst shrugged. "I am afraid, old fellow, the climber's cause is quite hopeless."

A martial light came into the duke's eyes. "We shall see," he said. "A war is not won in one battle."

Five

On waking the next morning, the duke decided that his determination of the day before to fight Miss Brigham's battles had been excessive. Really, the girl was none of his concern. He'd done what he could. He'd produced Lady Jersey. That, in itself, was an incredible feat! It was hardly his fault that, having had such an opportunity within her grasp, the little climber had failed to seize it. No. He had really done all he could.

Having had a late night of gambling (or was it early morning? He had not come in until five), the duke had lain abed until nearly noon. It took another hour for his valet to shave and dress him. Finally, at one o'clock in the afternoon, he went to his dining room in search of sustenance for the new day. In that stately room, he breakfasted on deviled kidneys, muffins, eggs, steak, and ale, and read *The Gazette*.

He was nearly finished when a footman

presented him with a note from his grandmother Whitworth. He read it and
scowled. Vouchers to Almack's must be
procured, the note informed him. And
while that was being done, Miss
Brightham's spirits must be kept up. All
manner of outings must be planned for
her amusement.

Really! Was it not enough he had been
trying desperately to get vouchers for the
female?, thought Littlefield, conveniently
forgetting the fact that he had wanted
those vouchers for his own wicked pur-
poses. He wasn't some lap dog with nothing to do but jump when his grandmother
snapped her fingers.

He thanked the footman, crumpled the
note, and pitched it over his shoulder. His
left shoulder. "For good luck," he said to
himself, and smiled, highly amused at his
own wit.

That afternoon, the Duke of Littlefield
went to see Mr. Stultz about a new coat.
He then went on to Tattersall's, where he
talked horseflesh and bought himself a
new mare. That night, splendid in evening
dress, he went to the King's Theatre
where, like the rest of the audience, he
ignored Madame Catalani and visited with
friends and acquaintances.

The following day, the note which arrived was dropped unopened into the fire and the duke went to Gentleman Jackson's boxing saloon. After an afternoon of boxing and visiting with other members of the Pugilistic Club, it was only natural that the duke move on to the Daffy Club, where the evening was pleasantly wasted drinking blue ruin and joining his friends in an enthusiastic, if off-key rendition of the club's official song.

Miss Brightham spent the evening playing cards with her grandmother and Mrs. Whitworth.

The next morning, the butler informed His Grace when he sat down to breakfast that Mrs. Whitworth's footman had come with a note for him and had instructions to wait for an answer.

The duke growled and stabbed his meat and told the butler to send the fellow in.

The footman was duly shown in. He handed over the note, respectfully telling His Grace that he had been instructed to say "Orphans" when handing over the missive.

The duke glared at him and opened the letter.

"I am sure I won't need to ask you again to give us the pleasure of your company," wrote his grandmother. "We will look forward to seeing you at two o'clock."

"Bah!" spat the duke, and the footman nervously shifted his weight from one foot to another. Littlefield sighed in resignation. "Tell Mrs. Whitworth that I shall be delighted to wait on her," he said to the man.

The footman left, and the duke returned to the important task of consuming his breakfast. He wondered if Miss Brightham had missed seeing him, then dismissed the thought as of no importance, turning his attention to what he would do with the rest of the day after paying his duty call on his grandmother. A bit of Bond Street lounging might be enjoyable. Perhaps Barncastle would like to accompany him. Old Barny was saying only the other day he was in desperate need of a new snuffbox. Littlefield himself could stand a visit to Fribourg and Treyer. And he was definitely in need of a new hat.

The word *hat* brought back an unbidden image of Miss Brightham in the milliner's shop, holding onto that bonnet with the ridiculous purple plume and looking longingly at it. Idly, Littlefield wondered if any more of her new clothes had come.

He presented himself at his grandmother's house promptly at two o'clock, a
vision in buff pantaloons and a bottle
green coat, his cravat as perfect and white
as new snow. His boots, by Hoby, had the
kind of shine only attainable by use of the
potion, *vin de champagne,* and much elbow
grease.

Mrs. Long burst into a gushing soliloquy
at the sight of him. His grandmother gave
him no such hero's welcome. "We are so
glad you could make time for us in your
schedule," she said with asperity.

The duke flushed. "I am afraid I have
been busy."

"I can well imagine," said his grandmother, her voice falsely sweet. "Never
mind that poor Miss Brightham has been
cooped up here with nothing to do for the
past two days."

Betsy jumped in quickly. "There is no
need to trouble the duke. I am quite content here with you."

Littlefield looked at her. Was she being
kind, trying to take his grandmother's fire?
Or was she trying, merely to pique him,
to pretend she had no interest in him?

"It is a lovely day," said Mrs. Whitworth.
"Why don't you take our guests to the
park."

"Betsy, love, I am sure you would enjoy

that. Would you not?" Mrs. Long trilled. "And I am sure it would be very good for Andrew to get out in the fresh air."

"We were out in the fresh air only yesterday, Grandmama," Betsy reminded her. "Don't you remember? I took Andrew for a walk."

"A little boy must have fresh air and exercise every day," said Mrs. Whitworth. "And I am sure the duke would be delighted to take you." The look she gave Littlefield told him he had better be delighted.

He smiled stiffly at Betsy. "It would be my pleasure," he said.

"Then, if you really don't mind," said Betsy, looking at him as if she meant to let him off the hook.

"Not in the least," he lied, then wanted to kick himself. Yet again, his grandmother had called the tune and he was dancing. Bond Street would not see the Duke of Littlefield this day.

Betsy sprang up. "I shall be ready in a trice. My new walking gown arrived only yesterday. And the white pelisse as well."

"And I shall ring for a servant to fetch Andrew," said Mrs. Long. "I am sure he is still in the kitchen making a nuisance of himself. Another reason to take the boy to the park, don't you know," she informed the duke. "He is always in the kitchen, begging treats from the cook. If he does not get more exercise he will become a roly-poly."

Littlefield smiled politely and wished he had sent a note to his grandmother telling her he had been called back to his country seat on urgent and unexpected business. Mrs. Long droned on, and he smiled and nodded, hearing nothing she said, watching the drawing-room door and waiting for his deliverance.

Andrew was the first to appear. He roared into the room like a strong wind and deluged Littlefield with questions. "Do we go in your curricle? Shall we go to Hyde Park again? I liked that ever so much. It is a very big park. May we bring some breadcrumbs to feed the birds?"

"You shan't go at all if you plan to chatter at me like that the whole time," warned Littlefield, and Andrew fell instantly silent and hung his head. "And yes, whelp, we shall go in my curricle," added Littlefield, removing the sting from his rebuke.

"Hooray!" whooped Andrew.

"Now, Andrew," scolded Mrs. Long. "What was the duke just telling you . . ."

Her voice faded to a background babble as the duke took in the sight that came through the drawing-room door. Brummell was right. Clothes did make the man. Or, in this case, the woman. Miss Brightham had never looked lovelier. The white of her pelisse seemed to bring out the creaminess of her skin, and her face looked nothing short of adorable, framed with curls and topped with her new poke bonnet. If she looked this enchanting in walking dress, what would she look like in the evening gown he had selected?

"I am ready," she said shyly.

"Then let us be off," he said jovially, all thought of Bond Street gone.

"Where is Andrew?" asked Betsy, looking around.

"Here I am!" piped Andrew, appearing out of nowhere.

Littlefield suddenly wished he hadn't agreed to take Andrew as well. He decided he would allow the boy to run on ahead as much as he liked.

And once set free on the great expanse of Hyde Park, Andrew took full advantage of the duke's generosity, running full tilt, first in one direction, then another.

Betsy turned to Littlefield and said, "It was so very good of you to bring us here. Andrew has not had this much room to romp since we came to London."

"It is my pleasure," said Littlefield.

"Is it?" she teased. Littlefield frowned

at having his generosity mocked, and she laughed. "Oh, Gabriel! You look so funny when you frown." This remark did nothing to make the duke smile, but Betsy seemed not to notice. She went on, "You have been so very good to us." She hesitated a moment, as if drawing her courage. "I want you to know that even though your grandmama expects you to help me make my way in society, I shan't be hurt if you don't."

The duke stared at her, his face registering both disbelief in her words and irritation at her perspicacity.

She blushed and let her gaze drift to follow Andrew across the park. "That is, it cannot be pleasant to be forced to entertain someone. And I am sure, after Lady Jersey's visit, even you could not procure vouchers to Almack's for Grandmama and I."

Here was another person telling him he was incapable of getting those curst vouchers! Littlefield found he was getting very tired of hearing about how incapable he was.

"I am not disappointed, anyway," Betsy continued. "Grandmama seems to think I have a right to move in exalted circles, but if the ladies of the ton are all like Lady Jersey, I think I'd as lief not."

"They are not all like Lady Jersey," the duke assured her. "And you may rest assured, I shall procure vouchers for you."

"How kind you are!" exclaimed Betsy. "Did ever a girl have a better guardian angel?"

"I wish you would stop referring to me as an angel," snapped Littlefield. "I have told you before, I am far from it."

"Yes, Your Grace," murmured Betsy, obviously hurt.

"And don't call me Your Grace in that servant tone," commanded the duke.

Betsy's mouth began to tremble. Tears pooled in her eyes.

This reaction was not lost on the duke, and he swore under his breath. She was going to make a scene. Right here in Hyde Park. "Here, now," he said nervously. "You don't mean to cry, do you?"

Betsy sniffed and replied in a wobbly voice, "No, Your Grace. I don't mean to."

Your Grace. It sounded so stiff, so formal, so full of fear.

"I did not mean to make you angry," said Betsy in a small voice. "I simply wanted you to know how grateful I was and how kind I thought you . . ." She broke off and bit her lip. A tear drizzled down her cheek, followed by another.

"Oh, here now," said the duke, digging

in his coat for a handkerchief. "You mustn't cry. People will think me the veriest beast."

"Oh, and you aren't," said Betsy, her voice still shaky. She took the proffered handkerchief and dabbed at her eyes. "I am impertinent." She looked at him earnestly. "But I did not mean to be," she added.

"I know," he said kindly.

"Your Grace!" Andrew's excited holler ended the conversation, and the pair looked to see him bounding across the park, accompanied by a big shaggy mongrel. "Look what I found!"

The animal joyously leapt first at Betsy, then the duke, succeeding in marking both with his dirty paws. "Down, you beast!" commanded Littlefield, whacking the dog on the nose.

"Oh, my new pelisse!" mourned Betsy.

"He didn't mean to get it dirty," said Andrew. "He's just friendly. I don't think he has a master. I have asked everyone in the park, and no one claims him. He must be an orphan." Andrew turned to Betsy. "May we give him a home?"

"Oh, Andrew. I am afraid not," said Betsy. "We can hardly bring the animal back to Mrs. Whitworth, who is already much crowded with all of us. It wouldn't be at all considerate."

"But he will starve," protested Andrew.

The dog sat on his haunches, his tongue hanging out, and looked hopefully at Littlefield.

"He is awfully thin," said Betsy sympathetically. She reached down and patted the dog. "Oh, my," she said, seeing the palm of her once-white glove now a light brown. "He is awfully dirty."

"The duke could keep him," suggested Andrew. "Your grandmama said you have a very big house. And you live in it all alone."

"I have eight servants," said Littlefield sternly. "That is hardly living alone."

"But you have no brother or sister, no grandmama. You must get lonesome," pointed out Andrew. "Whitey would make a nice friend."

"Whitey?" said Betsy.

"That is the name I have given him," Andrew informed her.

"You are an optimist," murmured the duke.

"And besides," Andrew continued, looking earnestly at Littlefield, "you need only keep him until our visit is done. Then we will take him home with us."

"Oh, my," said Betsy nervously.

"Father said I should have a dog," said Andrew stoutly.

"Yes, and he also said, 'But I don't know what we would do with one,'" quoted Betsy.

"And besides, this is no dog," put in Littlefield scornfully, thinking of the fine, well-behaved hunting dogs he kept at his lodge.

"Oh, Betsy. Please," pleaded Andrew. He knelt and put his arms around the dog's neck, and the animal licked him.

"Oh, very well," said Betsy. "That is, if the duke . . ." Here she stopped and looked at Littlefield, and it seemed to him the look on her face was nearly as pleading as the boy's.

He frowned. He was going to regret this. He knew it. "Very well," he said shortly. "But if this mongrel chews so much as one chair leg, he will be an orphan once more."

"Oh, thank you, Your Grace!" cried Andrew. He jumped up and hugged the duke fiercely, and the dog wagged his tail and barked.

The duke, finding himself feeling oddly heroic and embarrassed by it, gruffly said, "Here now. My clothes are already ruined enough without you crushing them, cub."

Andrew released his hold and beamed

up at the duke. He patted the animal's shaggy head. "There, Whitey. You are to have a home with a duke. You had best behave." To the duke he said, "He needs a bath. Will you help me give him one?"

"Certainly not," said Littlefield. "That is why one employs servants."

The fashionable hour of five o'clock was nearly upon them, and all manner of expensive equipages were appearing in the park. The duke decided it was time to leave before anyone saw him with his dirty clothes and the ridiculous animal. "Perhaps we should take Whitey home now," he suggested.

Betsy, too, was looking around the park and seeing the increased number of people strolling about. "Yes, I think that would be a good idea," she agreed.

Littlefield hustled them across the park and back to where his tiger was walking his horses. With unseemly speed, he hoisted both Betsy and Andrew into the curricle. To his tiger, he said, "Take the dog up in back with you."

But the tiger, it soon became evident, was unable to get the dog into the equipage, either by strength or coaxing.

"Come on, Whitey!" cried Andrew. "Come on! You can do it. Hop up!"

The duke swore, then called for his tiger

to come hold the reins. Tossing them down to him, Littlefield climbed down from the curricle and picked up the animal, who squirmed in his arms and got mud and dirt all over his coat. Littlefield hefted him up onto the curricle, brushed off his coat as best he could, and resumed his seat.

The dog surveyed the world from his perch and gave a hearty woof.

"Be quiet," snapped the duke, shoving the dog's drooling face away from his shoulder.

"I think he likes to ride in a curricle," announced Andrew.

"I am so glad," said Littlefield, "I, myself, like to look like a menagerie on wheels."

Betsy stifled a giggle.

Before they had gotten out of the park, the duke saw half a dozen of his acquaintance. When he introduced Betsy to Lady Dalrymple, her eyes shone with curiosity as she took in his dirty condition and his companions, especially the large shaggy one. But Littlefield did not, by word or action, betray the absurdity of his situation. "Miss Brightham is staying with my grandmother for the season," he said politely. Then to Betsy, "Lady Dalrymple is one of London's fairest flowers. We all wore black the day she married old Dalrymple."

"Oh, Your Grace," giggled the young matron. "Such a shameless flatterer you are!"

The duke looked at Lady Dalrymple in mock offense. "I? A flatterer? I assure you, I speak only the truth," he said.

"I am Andrew," piped up Andrew.

"Andrew!" scolded his sister. "He is my brother," she said to Lady Dalrymple.

"And a very pretty little boy he is," said her ladyship kindly.

"We have been to the park," explained Littlefield stupidly.

"So I see," said her ladyship, an amused smile on her face.

Littlefield smiled back, feeling ridiculous. "And now, if you will excuse us, we must be on our way."

"Certainly," said Lady Dalrymple. "It was so nice to have met you, Miss Brightham. I hope we shall meet again soon."

"Thank you," said Betsy, pleased.

"Drive on," Lady Dalrymple instructed her coachman, and with a final smile of amusement, she waved gaily.

The duke cracked his whip and the horses jumped forward. "Let us be out of here," he muttered under his breath. "If I must stop to speak to one more person in this condition, I shall go mad."

"Surely people see the dog and understand our dirty condition," said Betsy.

"People see that mongrel and think me ready for Bedlam," retorted Littlefield.

Betsy fell silent a moment. "Is Lady Dalrymple truly one of the most beautiful women in London?"

"Of course not," said the duke. He cast Betsy a sideways glance. "Surely you cannot have lived so sheltered a life that you know not when a man is simply flattering a lady because he knows she wishes it."

"Of course I know," replied Betsy huffily. She fell silent. After a few moments, she looked at the duke and asked, "Do you think I am pretty?"

"Now, why the devil are you pestering me with such questions?" responded Littlefield testily.

Betsy shrugged and looked away. "I simply wondered," she said. "Do you think Lady Dalrymple is pretty at all?"

"Of course she is pretty," said the duke. "I will allow her that."

"Am I as pretty as Lady Dalrymple?"

"Yes," he snapped. "Why *are* you asking me all these questions?"

"I simply wondered if I was pretty."

"Now that we have some decent clothes for you, you look quite fetching," said Littlefield. "I am sure you'll have no trouble snaring yourself a husband."

Somehow, this wasn't the right answer, for instead of looking pleased, Betsy sighed.

"Now what is wrong?" he demanded.

"Nothing," said Betsy stiffly.

"Come now. Out with it."

She brushed at a dirty spot on her gown. "I just thought perhaps you might say something to me such as you said to Lady Dalrymple. But of course, that was silly."

"Of course it was," agreed Littlefield. "After all, Lady Dalrymple is . . . Well, that is . . . Confound it! I am responsible for bringing you out. I have no need to flatter you."

"I see," said Betsy softly.

"Oh, you don't see at all," growled Littlefield.

"I think Betsy is pretty," put in Andrew, and his sister gave him a wistful smile and patted his arm.

"Here we are," announced Littlefield. He yanked on the reins with more force than usual, and the horses tossed their heads and pranced. His tiger jumped down to hold the horses' heads, and Littlefield helped his passengers out of the curricle. Whitey was disinclined to remain with the duke and jumped down from his perch. After much undignified chasing, the duke caught the animal by the scruff of the neck and hurled him back up into the curricle, an exercise which left His Grace scowling.

"Thank you for taking us to the park," said Andrew. "Take good care of Whitey. I shall come over as soon as I can to help give him a bath."

"If I have not slaughtered him first," muttered Littlefield.

"What did you say, Your Grace?" asked Andrew.

"I said, 'An excellent idea,'" replied Littlefield, still frowning.

"Thank you for giving up an afternoon for our entertainment," said Betsy. She looked at Littlefield's coat. "I am sorry about your coat," she added.

The duke shrugged. "It will clean," he said nobly. Somehow, he felt he should say more. Things were not how they should be.

What was he thinking? How the devil should things be, anyway? This girl was no relation to him, no real concern of his. Only see how she had upset him! His clothes were ruined. He would, most likely, be a laughingstock by tomorrow. And it was all because of this ridiculous female and her family. Here she was, looking at

him as if he were some sort of saint. Gads!
It was enough to sicken a man. "My horses
have been standing long enough," he said
shortly. "Good day, Miss Brigand." He
bowed over Betsy's hand, then jumped up
into his curricle and drove off without another glance at either Betsy or her brother,
the shaggy dog barking farewell.

"Why is the duke so angry?" asked Andrew.

"I am sure I don't know," snapped
Betsy, and she turned her back on the clat-
tering curricle and marched up the front
walk.

Six

Littlefield stomped into his townhouse, bellowing for his butler.

Well-bred man that he was, Macomber didn't blink an eye at the dirty mongrel that accompanied his employer. "Your Grace?"

"Take this beast and tether him out in back of the house. Tell Cook to give him some beefsteak and whatever soup bones he may have lying about."

"Yes, Your Grace," said the butler. He looked at the dog with a wary eye. "Come, boy," he tried.

The dog sat on his haunches and cocked his head.

The butler cleared his throat and tried again, but to no avail. Looking frustrated, he reached for the dog. Whitey growled.

The duke lost patience. He grabbed the animal by its furry neck, bringing out a surprised yelp, then proceeded to drag it off down the hall. "Come on, you filthy beast. You have caused me enough trouble this day."

The dog came reluctantly, and the butler followed at a safe distance. Once the kitchen had been reached, the duke issued his instructions himself. "And Macomber. I don't wish to see this animal again. Keep him out back. Tomorrow John and Abel may give him a bath."

"Where does Your Grace wish him to be bathed?"

"In the kitchen, I suppose," said the duke.

Cook let out a gasp. "Dog hairs in the food, Your Grace."

The duke threw up his arms. "Bathe the beast in my hip bath, bathe him in the water closet. I don't care the least where you bathe him as long as I don't have to hear it, see it, or in any way be a party to it! Is that clear?" he ended on a roar.

Macomber looked hurt by this undeserved tirade but, mindful of his position, merely inclined his head and said, "Certainly, Your Grace."

The duke turned and stomped off. He stopped at the dining room to pull out a bottle of port from inside the sideboard and pour himself a glass, then went to his room and rang for his valet. A bath was exactly what he needed himself.

A faint tickling on his hand caused him to look down. He glared at the black speck and tried to pick it off, but it jumped away. "Fleas!" he spat, and finally, exasperated beyond bearing with his life and this day in particular, he tore off his coat and hurled it across the room.

The duke remained at home that night, choosing solitude over possible ridicule, for he was sure by now the entire ton knew of the ridiculous sight he had presented on his expedition to the park. He played solitaire and drank heavily, and retired early at one in the morning to lie in his bed and wonder if, perhaps, he ought to accompany Miss Brightham to purchase a new walking ensemble to replace the one which had been dirtied. Perhaps something in apple green.

At three in the morning, the sound of a dog barking awakened him. Idly wondering who in the neighborhood had let their pug escape, he rolled over and dozed off only to be wakened again. That was a very large bark for such a small dog.

He sat up, the realization of whose dog was disturbing his sleep suddenly on him. He jumped from his bed and yanked the bellpull furiously. Then, not waiting, he pulled on his dressing gown and strode irritably out into the hallway, bellowing, "Macomber!"

The butler appeared, black breeches pulled on over his nightshirt, his nightcap still on his head. "Yes, Your Grace," he said in harried accents.

"Why is that dog barking?" demanded the duke.

"I don't know, Your Grace," replied the butler. "I have sent John to quiet him."

"Well, see that he does," commanded the duke and went back to his bed.

Half an hour later the barking began again, and the duke bounded out of bed, swearing. He jerked his door open and roared, "Macomber!"

Again, the butler appeared. "I am so sorry, Your Grace. John gave him more beefsteak and some water. He won't be quiet. I think he is lonely."

"Lonely!" echoed the duke. He ran his fingers through his hair. "Curse it all. We'll get no sleep tonight at this rate."

"I am sorry, Your Grace. Truly I am. We don't know what to do with him."

"Well, bring him inside," said the duke. "Take him in with you.

Macomber's eyes bulged. "If I might remind Your Grace? The dog does not care for me."

The duke strode past his butler, down the stairs, down the hallway, through the kitchen and outside. There he found the footman pleading with the barking animal to be quiet. An angry Zeus come down from Olympus, the duke planted himself in front of the animal. "Hush!" he ordered.

The dog stopped barking and thumped its tail. "You stupid cur," he told it. "I suppose the moment my back is turned you will start that wretched barking again."

The dog stood up and wagged its tail violently. Littlefield sighed. "Oh, very well," he said. "Come."

Whitey trotted after him, following him back through the house and up to his room.

"But I warn you," said Littlefield, pointing a menacing finger at the dog, "if so much as one flea leaves that worthless body of yours and finds its way onto me, you will be back on the streets tomorrow."

The dog lay down on the carpet in front of the duke's bed and rested its head on its paws, looking up at Littlefield.

"Humph," he said, and climbed into bed.

The next morning the Duke of Littlefield was sitting at his dining-room table, eating his breakfast and tossing pieces of bacon to the dog, when Macomber announced the arrival of a guest. "Master Andrew from your grandmother's house is here and says he has come to help you give . . . Whitey," the name was said with distaste, "a bath."

Littlefield sighed. "Send him in."

Andrew made his entrance. "Good morning, Your Grace," he said cheerily. "Whitey!" he exclaimed, falling on his knees to give the dog a hug. The dog rewarded him by licking his face, and Andrew laughed. "How is he? Is he enjoying his stay with you?"

"Vastly," said the duke. "So. You have come to help me give Whitey a bath, have you? Does your grandmama know where you are?"

"Oh, yes," replied Andrew. "And Mrs. Whitworth sent a footman to walk me here." He patted the dog. "I thought your servants might not want to bathe Whitey, so I came to help you."

Littlefield smiled. "Yes," he said. "I think, perhaps, they had rather not. Well," he said, resigned to his fate, "sit and have some breakfast with me and then we will have at it."

"Thank you!" exclaimed Andrew. "I am very fond of bacon."

* * *

Lord Amhearst stopped in to see the
Duke of Littlefield and found him back in
the kitchen, in his stocking feet, a faded
pair of pantaloons, and a shirt, its sleeves
rolled up to his elbows. He and a little boy
had some great, mangy-looking dog in a
large tub filled with sudsy water and were
scrubbing the animal. Little puddles lay
about the kitchen floor, and a servant
stood by, holding a bucket full of more
water.

"Ho! What is this?" he cried.

"Amhearst," said Littlefield casually.
"You are just in time to help us. Take off
your jacket and roll up your sleeves."

"Surely you jest," said his friend.

"It is great fun," put in the boy.

"I am sure it is," agreed his lordship
amiably. "However, I did not come dressed
for dog-washing, so I am afraid I shall
have to miss out on the fun. I hear you
were in Hyde Park yesterday," he said to
Littlefield.

"I was," replied the duke cautiously.

Lord Amhearst raised his eyebrows.
"This female must be an amazing creature
to reduce you to . . ." He gestured to the
wet animal and equally wet boy. ". . . this.
I can hardly wait to meet her. In fact, it
would be a most fortuitous thing if she

turned out to be handsome, for, alas, Fleurette and I—"

"Miss Brightham is no ladybird," said Littlefield in discouraging tones.

"What is a ladybird?" asked Andrew.

"Never mind," said Littlefield. He rose from the tub, grabbed a towel, and wiped his hands. "Andrew, I am going to leave this job for you to finish. Abel will help you. Whitey is to stay inside until he is dry, but you may come back and play with him this afternoon if you like." With that he ushered his friend out of the room.

"I hear the girl is rather taking. Of course, if you want her for yourself, you have only to say so," said Lord Amhearst amiably.

"I don't want her," snapped Littlefield. "What the devil are you here for, Amhearst?"

Unoffended, Lord Amhearst shrugged. "Do you go to the Lion's card party tonight?"

"Yes," said the duke in distracted tones.

"Excellent," approved Lord Amhearst. "From what I hear of your outing yesterday, you'll need some new togs. Care to visit Weston with me?"

"Hmmm?"

Lord Amhearst rolled his eyes. "Never

mind. I know poor company when I see it. I shall see you tonight."

That night at Lord Lyon's card party, Lord Amhearst observed, "Let us hope our friend will engage in the same wool-gathering as he was this morning. Then I shall leave here with plump pockets. And I must confess, my pockets are very much to let at the moment."

"Ha!" crowed Lord Lyon, whose tawny tresses and loud voice had earned him the nickname the Lion. "I told you that bit of muslin would cost you dearly in the end."

Amhearst shrugged. "She was less expensive than a wife."

"Hear, hear," said another man. He then took up the thread of conversation which Lord Lyon had lost. "And why was our dear duke so distracted this morning?"

Lord Amhearst broke into a wide grin, undeterred by his friend's threatening glare. "Why, he was washing a dog."

This statement produced raised eyebrows, barks of laughter, and murmurs of, "How droll."

"Curst nuisance, keeping a dog in the city," observed Lord Lyon, throwing out a card. "Makes one look quite ridiculous. Look at old Poodle Bing."

"You only dislike Bing's dog because he hoisted his leg on you," teased Lord Amhearst.

"That is more than enough reason," replied Lyon. He turned to Littlefield. "I suppose there was a reason you were doing such a freakish thing."

"Of course there was," Lord Amhearst answered for his friend. "And, as always, it is a female who is responsible."

"Who is the fortunate lady?" asked Lord Lyon.

Littlefield was blushing furiously now. "No one," he said.

"No one is quite correct," Amhearst agreed. "She is a little nobody sprung out from nowhere. Littlefield's grandmother, as usual, holds her fortune over his head and forces the poor old fellow to lend countenance to the chit."

Lord Lyon was intrigued. "Do tell us more."

Littlefield shrugged. "There is little more to tell. Except to say that Lady Jersey is not going to be so obliging as to give her vouchers for Almack's."

"So old Silence does not approve?" asked another man.

Here Lord Amhearst burst into laughter. "And I cannot imagine why," he said.

"I sense a story here," said Lyon.

"Oh, is there," said Amhearst, and proceeded to relate the events of Lady Jersey's call as they had been told to him by Littlefield.

And the duke did not find the story half so amusing as it had been when he had told it. Perhaps, he decided, that was because he looked ridiculous simply by his association with Miss Brightham and her family. By the time Lord Amhearst was done, Littlefield was scowling.

"Well, there's an end to it," said Lord Lyon callously. "You'll never get the girl into Almack's now."

Lord Amhearst shook his head. "A pity. Littlefield had such plans for her."

The duke slapped down his card. "I will get her into Almack's," he said.

"Come now, old fellow," said Amhearst. "There is no disgrace in defeat. Cut your losses and be done with it."

"I *will* get her into Almack's," repeated Littlefield forcefully.

"I shall lay you a pony you won't," said Lord Lyon.

"Done," said the duke, then wondered just exactly how he would go about winning this wager.

* * *

He was still pondering the difficulties of the situation the next morning when a note arrived from his grandmother. "Take my guests to Vauxhall," it commanded, "and give me some peace."

Vauxhall, eh? The duke pondered the many entertainments at the popular pleasure garden. For an instant, a vision of himself escorting Miss Elizabeth Brightham down the Dark Walk, the promenade that inspired so many stolen kisses, popped into mind.

He frowned. What a ridiculous notion! You need to find yourself a fresh bit of muslin, he told himself sternly. The lack of certain pleasures is affecting your brain.

It had been a while since the duke, tiring of his ballet dancer, had set her free to find a new protector. He had been about to embark on a dalliance with a charming demi-rep with raven black curls and a mole on her left shoulder when this business with the Brightham had begun.

He tried to visualize himself on the Dark Walk with the willing young demi-rep. But try as he would, he couldn't, for the dark curls insisted on lightening to gold, and the pouting little rosebud mouth bloomed into a lusciously full-lipped one.

The perfect nose shortened and became freckled, and there, in his mind, stood Miss Betsy Brightham, his nemesis.

"Bah!" he said in disgust. But he scribbled a note to his grandmother anyway. "I will take all but the crone," he wrote.

When the duke called at five o'clock that evening, Andrew was beside himself with joy, jumping up and down. "Will we see the lady with the plume in her hair walking on the tightrope?" he asked. "And the fireworks? Mrs. Whitworth said they set off fireworks."

"Yes, cub," said Littlefield. "Vauxhall has all manner of entertainments."

"Oh, here is our dear duke!" exclaimed Mrs. Long, coming down the stairs and pulling on a glove. She reached the foot of the stairs and smiled up at Littlefield. "We are all ready," she informed him. "It is so very kind of you to take us. Andrew has been beside himself ever since your invitation arrived."

The duke had forgotten about Mrs. Long. How he could have forgotten such a walking nightmare, he had no idea. But he knew after this day, he never would again.

His grandmother, coming behind the woman, seemed to know it as well and obviously took perverse pleasure in the knowledge. She presented her cheek for her grandson to kiss. "Such a dear boy," she murmered. "Always thinking of others." She reached up and patted his face, and he gave her a resentful smile.

"I know our little Betsy will have a season to remember thanks to your kindness, Your Grace," said Mrs. Long.

As if on cue, Betsy appeared. Her ensemble was all in shades of pink and made Littlefield think of icing on a cake and rose flavoring. Her reticule was the only part of the ensemble which offended his sensibilities, and he suspected it was one she had beaded herself. He frowned.

She halted on the stairs. "What is wrong?" she asked.

"That reticule," he said.

She looked at the bag and then questioningly back at the duke. "I thought it looked rather nice," she said in disappointment.

"Well, never mind," said Littlefield, not wanting to start out on a wrong foot. He remembered their last conversation. "You look very fetching in that outfit," he said kindly.

She blushed and smiled, and murmured, "Thank you," and the duke decided it was going to be a most enjoyable evening.

"But I must say, my dear," put in Mrs. Long, "now that I see the finished prod-

uct, I am afraid that the duke is quite
right about your reticule. Oh, I am sure
it is fine enough for Vauxhall, but for paying social calls it simply won't do. Betsy
made it herself," she informed the duke.
"She does like to keep busy, and I am sure
that is a most admirable quality in a wife.
Now we have but to produce some suitors
who can appreciate such qualities. Of
course, I am sure we will have no trouble
finding suitors aplenty once our dear duke
has procured vouchers for Almack's," she
announced to the company in general.

The duke changed his prediction. Even
if they left Vauxhall immediately after the
Cascade at nine (which they would as-
suredly have to do in order to get Andrew
home and in bed, thank God), it was going
to be a very long evening.

Unless, by some stroke of genius, Littlefield could induce Mrs. Long to watch over
Andrew and leave him and the girl free
to enjoy themselves in peace. He smiled
wickedly. Yes, that was what he would do!
The two pests could take care of each
other. Much cheered, the duke smiled and
said, "Well then, let us be off."

"Enjoy yourself," called his grandmother sweetly.

"Oh, we shall," called back Mrs. Long.
"It has been many years since I have been

to Vauxhall," she informed Littlefield as they settled into his carriage. "I am sure much has been added." She turned to Andrew. "You may count yourself fortunate, young man, that the duke has been kind enough to allow you along on this outing. I am sure not many little boys are as indulged as you, to be allowed out with the grownups and without even your nurse along. We should have brought his nurse to watch over him," she continued in an aside to the duke as they rolled off down the street, "but the wretched creature is in bed with what she claims is a putrid sore throat. Ah well, how much trouble can one small boy be?"

How much indeed? thought Littlefield, remembering their outing to Hyde Park. The child was certainly overindulged. If he were in Littlefield's care, he should be seen to properly, taken out every day by a governess and exercised until he was too tired to make mischief. When he was older, he would be put under the care of a tutor until he was of an age to be sent to school. That, everyone knew, was the proper way to raise boys. Not this indulgent dragging them about everywhere as if they were lap dogs.

The duke thought of how little he'd seen of his parents before their death and

suddenly felt an odd stab of something re-
markably like jealousy.

"Andrew, you will behave yourself like a
good boy, won't you?" Mrs. Long was saying.

"Oh, yes, Grandmama," said Andrew
earnestly.

Mrs. Long smiled at her grandson, satisfied.

But once they got to Vauxhall, Andrew
forgot his resolution. Excited and heedless
of his grandmother's command to hold
her hand, he rushed ahead of everyone,
down the entrance avenue, and was swal-
lowed up in the crowd.

"Oh, dear!" cried Betsy in alarm.

Littlefield ground his teeth and took off
after the child. He caught Andrew fifty
feet down the Grand Walk and grabbed
him by the back of his jacket. "Here,
now," he growled. "Is this how you behave
and mind your grandmama?"

Andrew looked at him wide-eyed and
gulped.

Without waiting for an answer, the duke
hoisted the little boy under his arm and
strode back through the throng to the two
women. He set Andrew back on the
ground and squatted down in front of him
so they were face to face. "Now," said Littlefield slowly, "I don't intend to spend the

entire evening chasing after a whelp who is only here because his grandmother is soft-hearted." And soft-headed, he added mentally. "If you run ahead of your grandmother again, we shall go home immediately. Do you understand?"

Andrew bit his lip, sniffled and nodded.

"Good," said Littlefield, rising. "Now," he said to Mrs. Long, assuming his most commanding air, "you may take Andrew to the Hermit's Walk if you like, and I shall—"

"Oh, Your Grace," interrupted Mrs. Long, "I don't think it is a good idea to separate ourselves. Not at all. For if I were to lose Andrew in this crowd, I should not have the foggiest notion how to go about finding him."

"Which is exactly why children should not be dragged along on an adult outing," snapped the duke.

"Oh, you are so right," agreed Mrs. Long, and her toadying angered him even more. "I can see it was a very big mistake to bring Andrew," she rushed on. "But here we are and what can we do but make the best of it? And Your Grace is so very capable. I know if we all stay together nothing will happen."

It certainly won't, thought the duke irritably, seeing an enjoyable interlude far

down the Dark Walk vanish with a poof.
His eyes strayed to Betsy. She was looking
at him, her face at once pleading and re-
pentant. "Oh, very well," he said crossly.
"Let us all go to the Hermit's Walk."

"Hooray!" shouted Andrew, and immediately began tugging on his grandmother's arm. "Hurry, Grandmama."

They all went down the Hermit's Walk
and admired the transparency of the
seated hermit before his hut. Betsy pronounced it charming, and for some ridiculous reason, the duke found her enjoyment
pleased him.

After this, Andrew declared himself
starving, so the duke took a supper box,
and they feasted on ham, pigeon pie, and
chicken.

"I suppose in being here with us you
are giving up a fine dinner at some great
house tonight," ventured Betsy.

The duke shrugged and said nothing.

Betsy's gaze roamed the crowd that
passed by their box. "So many people here
tonight. So many people in London." She
sighed. "All these people, and yet I sometimes feel so very much alone. Except, of
course, when you are with us," she added,
smiling at Littlefield.

"Never you mind, lambkin." said her
grandmother. "Once the duke has pro-

cured those vouchers to Almack's, you will have more invitations than you know what to do with, I assure you."

The vouchers. For a while Littlefield had forgotten about them. How the devil was he going to win that wager, anyway?

Andrew popped the last thin slice of ham in his mouth and announced, "I want to go see the lady on the tightrope."

The duke pulled his watch from his waistcoat pocket. "She should be appearing soon."

"Then let us hurry," said Betsy, "for I confess, I am as excited to see her as Andrew."

They had barely left the supper box when Andrew, in the excitement of anticipation, forgot his promise to the duke and broke free of his grandmother's restraining grasp. "Andrew!" she cried. "Come back at once."

The boy rushed on, darting through the press of bodies.

Again, the duke gave chase. But this time he couldn't spot Andrew. He went to the spot where Madame Saqui was to appear and searched in vain for a small curly head. "Andrew!" he roared, and succeeded only in having people stare at him inquisitively.

Betsy and her grandmother searched as

well, stopping passersby to inquire if they
had seen a little curly-headed boy. At last,
a woman informed Betsy she had seen a
little boy being led off by a tall skinny man
in a patched coat. Betsy blanched. On
shaky legs, she ran to her grandmother
and grabbed her arm. "Grandmama," she
gasped, "Andrew has been kidnapped!"

Seven

Mrs. Long's face drained of blood. She swayed and grabbed at her granddaughter's arm.

"Grandmama!" cried Betsy in alarm.

The old woman took a deep breath. "We must find the duke," she said, her voice weak.

Betsy spied a bench off to one side of the walk. "Here, darling, you sit down and I shall fetch him." She had just gotten her grandmother settled and turned to run in search of Littlefield when he appeared on the walk, a frazzled expression on his face. "Oh, Gabriel!" cried Betsy, rushing to him. "Andrew has been kidnapped!"

"Kidnapped!" echoed Littlefield. "The deuce!"

"He has," insisted Betsy. "A woman saw him being led off by a skinny man in a patched coat."

Littlefield felt himself suddenly wrapped in ice. "Dear God," he said.

"What shall we do?"

"Let me think," he said, pressing his fingers to his forehead. He tried to imagine who could want a little boy like Andrew. Little. Of course . . . a chimney sweep! The duke ground his teeth. Where would the fellow go? Where else could he go but back down the entrance avenue, the Grand Walk. Littlefield took off at a run, Betsy following behind.

He ran the distance as if the devil himself were behind him, dodging strolling ladies and gentlemen, searching frantically as he ran, hoping for some sign of a struggling little boy and a skinny man. He saw only a blur of staring faces.

As he approached the entrance, he heard a high voice piping, "Let me go!"

"Andrew!" he called.

"Your Grace!" shrilled the child.

The duke swam through the crowd and surfaced to see a wriggling Andrew tucked under his kidnapper's arm. Littlefield called the child's name again, and the man dropped him and ran.

Freed, Andrew ran to the duke, who caught the sobbing child up in his arms. The villain had already vanished, so Littlefield concentrated his energies on Andrew. "Now, young man, you see why we told you to stay with us," he scolded.

"The man said he knew where I could find you," sobbed Andrew. "But he was going to take me out of the park. I said I wouldn't leave, I wanted to see the lady on the tightrope, and he . . . he . . . hit me."

Holding her side, Betsy arrived. "Oh, Andrew!" she gasped.

"Betsy," he cried and held out his arms to his sister.

The duke gave him over and watched while she hugged the little boy. She set him down and knelt before him. "Andrew, we were so worried," she said.

"I want to go home," Andrew sobbed.

Littlefield was sure the events of the past half-hour had aged him ten years, and he found he shared the boy's sentiments.

Betsy rose and held out her hand and the child took it meekly. "You did not catch the man who tried to steal him?" she asked Littlefield.

He shook his head. "The fellow saw me and bolted."

"Who would want to do such a thing?" demanded Betsy.

"A chimney sweep," guessed the duke. "They need boys little enough to climb up into the chimneys. Andrew is just the right size."

Betsy bit her lip. A tear slipped out the corner of her eye, and Littlefield felt a

sudden urge to put his arm around the
girl and comfort her. Irritably, he pushed
the feeling aside. The foolish chit had insisted on bringing the child along. He
should have been left home in bed, then
none of this would have happened.

"May we go home now?" Andrew asked
his sister.

"Certainly," she said. "We shall just fetch
Grandmama, and then we shall leave."

And I shall go on to Brooks's and re-
deem what is left of my evening, decided
the duke.

Mrs. Long burst into noisy tears at the
sight of her grandson. "How brave our
duke is," she said after hearing the story of
Andrew's rescue. "And how fortunate that
he was with us. Else our poor little Andrew
might have had a very grim future."

"It was nothing," said the duke mod-
estly, offering Betsy his arm.

"You truly are our guardian angel," said
Betsy, looking at him worshipfully.

This made Littlefield blush. What ridiculous drivel! If any of his friends ever
heard the girl talk like that, he would
never live it down. "Nonsense," he said.

He delivered his troublesome charges
back to his grandmother and, feeling like
a man escaped from Newgate, proceeded
to St. James's Street. Once there, he saun-

tered into Brooks's to wipe away, at the Faro table, all memories of domesticity.

As he sat down to gamble on his expectancies, he was still being thoroughly discussed at his grandmother Whitworth's townhouse. "I vow," said Mrs. Long to her old friend. "I cannot even remember what our life was like before your charming grandson became a part of it."

"He is a good boy," said Mrs. Whitworth, basking in the reflected glory of her grandson's chivalry.

"Just the right age to be thinking of setting up his nursery," continued Mrs. Long casually.

Mrs. Whitworth frowned. "One noble deed does not a husband make," she pointed out. "I am afraid Lionel has been very spoilt. He thinks of his own pleasures before all else."

"And what man does not?" countered Mrs. Long.

"To us he has been most generous with his time," put in Betsy, and Mrs. Whitworth bit her lip. Betsy looked closely at her hostess. Mrs. Whitworth ducked the prying gaze, inspecting the large ruby ring on her finger. "Perhaps," Betsy said slowly, "His Grace has been persuaded to devote so much time to us?"

"Lionel does what he wishes," asserted

Mrs. Whitworth. "It has been a long evening. I think we could all do with a good night's sleep."

"Yes, yes," agreed Mrs. Long. "An excellent idea, my dear Jane." She rose stiffly. "I must confess the events of this night have drained me. I feel a hundred years old. Good night, my child."

Betsy kissed her cheek and her grandmama made her way off to her room. Betsy was about to follow suit when Mrs. Whitworth said, "Betsy. A moment, if you please?"

Betsy turned.

Mrs. Whitworth came to stand next to her. "I would not have your heart broken, child," she said softly.

"I know," murmured Betsy. She patted Mrs. Whitworth's arm. "Thank you. For all you have done for us."

"I have done little enough, I am afraid," sighed Mrs. Whitworth. "But if Lionel can procure vouchers for Almack's, I will feel I have done well by your grandmama. And you will see there are many finer fish in the sea than the Duke of Littlefield."

Betsy nodded politely, then with a great sigh went to find her bed.

The Duke of Littlefield did not find his bed until the first feeble promise of dawn touched the London sky. His valet helped him off with his boots, then he dismissed the man, flopping onto his bed fully clothed to sleep off the effects of too much port and the loss of too much money.

It was in this weakened state Miss Betsy Brightham found him. "Dear Gabriel," she murmured. "I owe you a great debt for saving Andrew. I have never known a man braver, nor one more deserving of reward." She climbed onto the bed and snuggled next to him, kissing his cheek, teasing his ear with her tongue. Of course, being a gentleman, he tried to push her away, but she was insistent, forcing herself against him, becoming more and more abandoned in her kisses. Like some she-wolf, she laid a hand on his chest and licked his chin.

The duke opened his eyes. Round black eyes stared lovingly into his, and a giant pink tongue ran the length of his cheek. "Faugh!" spat the duke, and pushed the shaggy dog from him. "Who let you into my room, mongrel?"

The dog sat on its haunches, its tongue lolling, panting happily.

Littlefield shoved the animal off his bed and ran his fingers through his hair. Curse the chit! Wasn't it bad enough she plagued his waking hours? Must she also invade his dreams? Well, if she was going to occupy so much of his time, he would make it worth his while. He would quit procrastinating, get those vouchers straight away, and see some sport before another week had passed.

To that end he went to see his grandmother Hopewell. "I suppose you have come about that child and her odious family," she guessed.

The duke looked hurt as he fell onto the sofa. "Cannot a fellow come to see his own grandmother with no reason save to enjoy the pleasure of her company?"

"Not this fellow," said the dowager duchess.

Littlefield leaned forward and said earnestly, "You must help me. I am afraid circumstances did not work in favor of Miss Brightham and led Lady Jersey to form a wrong opinion—"

"I have heard the particulars of Lady Jersey's call, as have a great many ladies of the ton," interrupted Her Grace. "To help the girl now is quite impossible."

"Surely not for you," said her grandson.

"There is nothing I can do, Lionel. As if any of those ladies would listen to me, an old woman whose own son married beneath him."

Littlefield frowned. How his grandmother had sung a different tune on his last visit. "What of the favor her ladyship owes you?" he chided.

"*Some* things one simply cannot ask," replied his grandmother. "I tell you, it is hopeless. Lady Jersey has said nay, and if she disapproves . . ." The dowager duchess shrugged heartlessly.

"But that is ridiculous," objected Littlefield. "Do you mean to tell me that once Lady Jersey has made a decision no one dare cross her?"

"They don't call her Queen Sarah for no reason," replied Her Grace.

"Queen Sarah." The duke tapped his chin. "Perhaps," he mused, "some of her loyal subjects are becoming tired of her rule."

His grandmother stared at him. "Lionel. What devilish plan are you hatching?" she asked suspiciously.

"How can I know until it springs from its shell?" he replied with a smile, and took his leave.

While shopping for a new snuffbox at Friebourg and Treyer, the duke encountered Lord Amhearst, who asked how his battle for the vouchers progressed.

"Oh, fine," said Littlefield airily.

"And when will we see the fair climber at Almack's?" persisted Amhearst.

"Soon," replied Littlefield evasively.

Amhearst grinned and teased, "You are fighting a losing battle, you know."

"We shall see," said Littlefield.

"Do you come to my sister's come-out ball?" asked Lord Amhearst, changing the subject.

"The Flower knows I would not miss her come-out for love nor money," said Littlefield.

"If you call her by that name, she will wilt in front of the entire ton," predicted Amhearst.

"Now that she is out of the schoolroom, she no longer wishes to be teased, eh?"

"She considers herself grown up," said Amhearst. He shook his head. "The airs she has been putting on! Considers herself quite the society miss."

"Wait until the first man speaks to her," predicted Littlefield.

His friend nodded. "Poor thing. How she came to be so shy of men, I cannot imagine."

If Lady Amhearst had been present, she would have informed the two young men that their merciless teasing of Lady Hyacinth ever since she was a little girl had a great deal to do with that young lady's present nervousness.

"Well, I shall give her a dance," said Littlefield generously. "That should start the snowball rolling."

"Fair enough," said his friend. "After I lead her out for the first dance, I depend on you to take her for the quadrille."

"Tell her I have begged her to save it for me."

"Much she will believe that," scoffed Amhearst. "Here now. Here is a fine-looking snuffbox. I say, if you don't want it, I think I shall purchase it for myself. Damn if I won't."

Lady Hyacinth's ball was more than a social obligation to the Duke of Littlefield. It was the field where he would do battle for vouchers to Almack's for Miss Elizabeth Brightham. He arrived resplendent in a double-breasted *corbeau*-colored coat and light sage green breeches. His fine leg showed to advantage in silk stockings, and his feet were elegantly shod with black patent-leather pumps, each decorated with a small diamond buckle. A diamond stickpin glittered in his cravat. He folded his chapeau bras and tucked it under his arm, then went up the steps to the Amhearst townhouse, touching a hand to his carefully pomaded locks to make sure they were still in place.

Allow us to proposition you
in a most provocative way.

PRESENTING AN IRRESISTIBLE OFFERING ON YOUR KIND OF ROMANCE.

Receive 3 Zebra Regency Romance Novels (An $11.97 value)
Free

Journey back to the romantic Regent Era with the world's finest romance authors. Zebra Regency Romance novels place you amongst the English *ton* of a distant past with witty dialogue, and stories of courtship so real, you feel that you're living them!

Experience it all through 3 FREE Zebra Regency Romance novels...yours just for the asking. When you join *the only book club dedicated to Regency Romance readers,* additional Regency Romances can be yours to preview FREE each month, with no obligation to buy anything, ever.

Regency Subscribers Get First-Class Savings.

After your initial package of 3 FREE books, you'll begin to receive monthly shipments of new Zebra Regency titles. These all new novels will be delivered direct to your home as soon as they are published...sometimes even before the bookstores get them! Each monthly shipment of 3 books will be yours to examine for 10 days. Then, if you decide to keep the books, you'll pay the preferred subscriber's price of just $3.30 per title. That's $9.90 for all 3 books...a savings of over $2 off the publisher's price! What's more, $9.90 is your total price. (A nominal shipping and handling charge of $1.50 per shipment will be added.)

No Minimum Purchase, and a Generous Return Privilege.

We're so sure that you'll appreciate the money-saving convenience of home delivery that we <u>guarantee</u> your complete satisfaction. You may return any shipment...for any reason...within 10 days and pay nothing that month. And if you want us to stop sending books, just say the word. There is no minimum number of books you must buy.

Say Yes to 3 Free Books!

COMPLETE AND RETURN THE ORDER CARD TO RECEIVE THIS $11.97 VALUE. ABSOLUTELY FREE.

(If the certificate is missing below, write to: Zebra Home Subscription Service, Inc., 120 Brighton Road, P.O. Box 5214, Clifton, New Jersey 07015-5214

3 FREE BOOKS

Yes! Please send me 3 Zebra Regency Romances without cost or obligation. I understand that each month thereafter I will be able to preview 3 new Regency Romances FREE for 10 days. Then, if I should decide to keep them, I will pay the money-saving preferred subscriber's price of just $9.90 for all 3...that's a savings of over $2 off the publisher's price. (A nominal shipping and handling charge of $1.50 per shipment will be added.) I may return any shipment within 10 days and owe nothing, and I may cancel this subscription at any time. My 3 FREE books will be mine to keep in any case.

Name _____

Address_____ Apt. _____

City_____ State_____ Zip_____

Telephone ( ) _____

Signature _____
(If under 18, parent or guardian must sign.)   RP1294

Terms and prices subject to change. Orders subject to acceptance by Zebra Home Subscription Service, Inc.

Inside, he took his place in the receiving line to await his turn to thank his hostess for inviting him to this terrible crush and to compliment the Flower on how well she looked. He murmured a polite greeting to the acquaintance in front of him and wondered how Elizabeth would show in a crowd such as this.

He flicked a casual eye over two young ladies standing further up the line with their mamas and papas. Actually, they were no better looking than Elizabeth, he decided. Dressed in her new ballgown, she could certainly give them a run for their money. He smiled. It was going to be such a lark to set her against the likes of them and see who snagged a husband first.

Of course, old Bacon wasn't much of a husband. But for someone with no connections, he was a fine catch.

For some odd reason, the thought of Betsy with the fat lord produced a frown. The duke gave himself a mental shake. What the devil was wrong with him these days, anyway?

The line moved slowly, but at last he found himself greeting his old friend, bowing over Lady Amhearst's hand and then Lady Hyacinth's. "I hope your brother gave you my message, Little Flower," he teased.

Lady Hyacinth's fair skin turned a deli-

cate pink, and she lowered her gaze and
nodded.

"Excellent," said the duke. "I shall seek
you out."

"Thank you, Your Grace," she whispered, and Littlefield thought what a mouse
she had become.

When he danced with her, she was all
blushes and monosyllables. By the time the
music had ended, Littlefield felt quite fatigued. Really. How exhausting it was trying to make conversation with a female too
nervous to converse! He hoped, for his
friend's sake, the Flower would find her
footing soon. Else she would become a
wallflower. He would have to talk to old
Amhearst about that. Perhaps Amhearst
could coach her. Elizabeth could certainly
teach her a thing or two about how to hold
a gentleman's interest.

The thought of Miss Brightham caused
him to search the room for his quarry. He
soon spied Lady Cowper sitting on a gilt
edged chair on the opposite side of the ballroom, speaking with a turbaned dowager.

He approached her ladyship, bowed low,
and begged the honor of the next dance.
"I believe it is a waltz. Does your ladyship
have permission to dance it?"

Lady Cowper was a lovely woman with a
reputation for wit and kindness. She

laughed appreciatively at the duke's jest. Young ladies making their come-out required the permission of one of Almack's patronesses to experience the scandalous waltz. "I think I may safely indulge myself," she replied. "And I shall, indeed, feel I am indulging myself to take the floor with such a handsome man, Your Grace."

The duke smiled and acknowledged the compliment with a slight bow. He held out his arm to her, and she took it and allowed him to lead her onto the floor.

"I think I might guess the reason for the kind attentions of the Duke of Littlefield," she said.

"Might you?" he responded. "Pray, don't tell your husband for I should hate to have him call me out."

Her small full lips fell into a playful smile. "It will do you no good, you know."

"Then it is true?" responded the duke. "Queen Sarah rules the committee completely, and none but her have power?"

Lady Cowper gave him an arch look. "Is that what you think?"

"Is that not what all the ton thinks?" replied Littlefield.

Lady Cowper fell silent, and the duke sensed his words had had some effect. He pressed his advantage. "Of course, I have also heard that your ladyship is the kindest of the patronesses."

"She is not ton," said her ladyship, cutting to the heart of the issue.

"She is not lowborn," said the duke. "In fact, her parentage does not disgrace her," he continued, stretching the truth taut.

"Who is her family?" retorted Lady Cowper.

"Who is my family?" Littlefield argued.

Her ladyship looked at him speculatively. "You fight well for your lady, Sir Knight."

The duke wanted to protest that Miss Brightham was not his lady, but wisely kept his mouth shut.

Lady Cowper smiled at him. "I shall see what can be done," she said, and the Duke of Littlefield smiled graciously and thanked her, all the while envisioning the Lion paying him a call to hand over his blunt and commend him for his cleverness. Great sport, this business of bringing out a female!

Eight

There was much excitement the following Monday when the duke arrived at his grandmother Whitworth's with the all-important vouchers in hand.

"Lord bless us!" exclaimed Mrs. Long, clasping the papers to her ample bosom. "He got them!" She smiled up at Littlefield as if he were a saint. "I knew if anyone could procure such a treasure for my little Betsy, it was Your Grace," she said. "Oh, and won't she be thrilled! Such a kind man. Such a kind and noble man!" And without waiting to ring for a servant, Mrs. Long rushed from the drawing room, calling for her granddaughter to come down quickly and only see what the Duke of Littlefield had accomplished on her behalf.

"Well, Lionel. I congratulate you," said his grandmama. "After Lady Jersey's unfortunate visit, I thought we were lost, indeed."

"And then you should have been rid of

them," teased Littlefield. "Now you are trapped for the season."

Mrs. Whitworth sighed. "If I could find a way to send my dear friend and her Mama and grandson home, I should not mind if Betsy remained indefinitely, for she is, indeed, a dear child. And if goodness alone may be rewarded, then I hope she makes a fine match."

"I can promise you, dearest, I shall do everything in my power to ensure she makes the splendid match of which you find her so deserving," murmured Littlefield.

Mrs. Whitworth looked sharply at him, but the face looking back at her was bland and innocent. "See that you do, young jackanapes," she said shortly.

At that moment, Mrs. Long fluttered back into the room, Betsy in her wake. "Ah, here sits our kind benefactor with such a modest countenance!" exclaimed Mrs. Long. "Heaven alone knows to what lengths he has gone on our behalf."

Betsy smiled at their kind benefactor, who rose and bowed over her hand. "We truly are grateful," she said simply. "Does this mean I am now ton?"

"Of course it does," said her grandmother. "Now we must attend Almack's this Wednesday evening, so all the eligible nobles may see what a fine catch has arrived in London." She looked playfully at the duke. "And perhaps our dear duke would escort us?"

Their dear duke said that, indeed, he would be delighted to do so, for their dear duke had his own particular plans for Miss Brightham.

There was little enough that could be said about the building that housed Almack's Assembly Rooms. Its brickwork exterior was judged plain. The ballroom was a huge, spare room, and its dance floor was considered poor. No one entered those sacred portals for either the food, which was also considered poor, nor the gambling, as the stakes were boringly low.

But to Miss Betsy Brightham, who now stood on the threshold of social success, the assembly rooms were nothing short of wonderful. She looked at the men in their knee breeches and dress coats, and the ladies in their finery, and felt she had never in her life seen such a glittering and impressive gathering.

"Do take that look off your face," chided the duke. "You are not a child entering Gunther's for the first time."

"But it is all so wonderful," said Betsy breathlessly. "I am sure you must take this all for granted because you are accustomed to it, but to me it is all very exciting." Not for the first time, she asked him, "Will I do?"

"Of course you will do," he snapped. Betsy looked hurt by his sharpness, and it irritated him that he now felt badly for having been short with her. To make them both feel better, he added, "I told you that seafoam green was a perfect color for you when we first visited the dressmaker." He even went so far as to add, "It complements your hair."

"Oh, do you really think so?"

She looked so eager, so thrilled. Littlefield smiled. Foolish chit. "Yes, Elizabeth," he said, his voice gentled. "I really think so. Now. I suppose you would like some punch?"

"Oh. Don't leave me," she begged. "I should be terrified."

"Very well," he said. "Would you care to dance?"

She looked only slightly less nervous at the prospect of dancing than she had at being left alone at the side of the ballroom. "I suppose," she said doubtfully.

Littlefield caught sight of Sir Harry Bacon on the other side of the room, eyeing the crowd casually. He had told old Bacon he would be here tonight with the lovely

Miss Brightham. And she did, indeed, look lovely. Bacon couldn't help but be smitten, especially as he was already inclined to be so, believing Miss Brightham to be an heiress. "Come," said Littlefield. "Sets are forming for the quadrille."

Betsy smiled nervously and let the duke lead her out onto the floor. She smiled at the other couples as Littlefield presented her, and the duke nodded his encouragement as the music started and they began the first figure. He noticed that her nervousness remained for some time, but by the second figure she seemed to relax; her smiles became more confident.

Toward the end of the second figure, however, she began to behave oddly. She let out a tiny yelp and lifted her foot as if she'd stepped on a pebble. What odd start was this? wondered Littlefield irritably. It seemed less than a moment when the action was repeated. As soon as the movements of the dance allowed him to get close, he hissed, "What ails you?"

"I stepped on something," she replied.

"Nonsense," he said. "There is nothing here on which to step but smooth wood."

"It felt like a pebble," she insisted.

"This is not the beach," Littlefield informed her. "Quit hopping about. You are making a cake of yourself."

She looked at him in dismay. "Oh, dear," she fretted.

They parted, but when next they came together, something small and round skittered under Littlefield's slippered foot, causing him to misstep. He had no sooner recovered his balance when another something slipped under him.

Betsy looked at the floor. "My slippers!" she cried.

Two more little beads rolled underfoot, causing Littlefield to add an interesting new hop to the dance. Their fellow dancers stared at him as if he had run mad. He felt a warm blush infusing his face.

"The beads have come loose from my slippers," moaned Betsy.

The duke forced a smile for their fellow dancers.

"What shall we do?" Betsy hissed over the music.

"Watch where we step and hope no one else encounters the curst beads," instructed Littlefield.

By the fourth figure, beads lay like tiny hailstones about the dancers, and ladies and gentlemen alike were slipping and windmilling their arms as if they danced on ice. Snickers rose like mist from all corners of the ballroom, then evolved into belly laughs, and titters behind lacy fans.

Red-faced, the gentlemen gave up the farce and led their ladies from the floor. A tight-lipped duke escorted Betsy to a chair and watched while a servant rushed to sweep up the menacing little decorations.

Betsy pointed a slipper out in front of her. Except for a single bead that clung stubbornly, there was now nothing on it but threads.

Littlefield looked down at it and scowled. "You shall have to return those," he said. "First thing in the morning."

"But I cannot," said Betsy, distressed.

"Well, you certainly cannot let merchants get by with foisting shoddy workmanship on you. Anyway, there is nothing to returning a pair of slippers. If you like, I shall send them back. I know how to handle these things."

"But you cannot," insisted Betsy.

"I most certainly can," said the duke in lofty tones.

"Not these," said Betsy in a small voice. "I made them."

"What!" boomed the duke, then feeling eyes on him, settled his ruffled feathers and forced a smile onto his face. "What happened to the slippers my grandmother purchased for you?" he demanded, smiling at any and all.

"They were never delivered. And I didn't wish to make a fuss . . ."

"So instead you made a scene."

"It was not my intent to make a scene," said Betsy stiffly.

"I suppose those beads are yet another sample of your handiwork," said the duke scornfully. Before she could answer, he continued, "That hideous bonnet was an affront to the eyes, but at least it did not endanger life and limb."

"Oooh," growled Betsy.

"Don't go flying up in the boughs here in front of the whole world," cautioned the duke in frigid accents.

"This is not the whole world," said Betsy haughtily.

"It is the whole civilized world," said Littlefield. "And you had best remember that. You won't make any kind of marriage pulling tricks like this."

Betsy shrugged. "Then I suppose I shan't make a fine marriage."

Littlefield gave her a reproving look, and she raised an eyebrow, daring him to say more. "You must be dicked in the nob," he grumbled at last. "Whoever heard of a female not wanting to make a fine marriage?"

"Oh, I would like to be married," said Betsy. "But I should like to be happily married to a man who cares for me and who wants to share his life with me; someone with whom I can laugh."

"That is why you have friends," said Littlefield impatiently.

"I should like my husband to be my friend," said Betsy in a small voice.

Her lower lip began to tremble, and she caught it between her teeth. Here was a sign of impending tears, thought Littlefield, and a feeling of panic settled on him. "Here now," he pleaded. "There is no need to cry."

"There is every need to cry," she informed him, her voice warning him that a shower of tears was impending.

"My dear duke," said a gentle voice at his side, and Littlefield jumped. "Oh, Lady Cowper," he said nervously. Recovering himself, he stood and bowed over her hand. "It is so good to see you."

"And it is so very good to see the lovely young lady I have sponsored. May I have an introduction?"

Littlefield did the honors, and Betsy managed to rise and give her ladyship a curtsy and a teary smile. "It was so very kind of your ladyship . . ." She got no further before her voice broke.

"There now," said Lady Cowper, taking her arm and seating them both in chairs.

"Such on embarrassing thing could happen to any one of us. I recommend you return those slippers first thing in the morning."

"Oh, she intends to," said Littlefield before Betsy could say anything, and she looked at him, obviously not grateful that he had answered for her.

Lord Amhearst now stood before them, begging an introduction. Lady Cowper obliged, and on seeing Betsy safely launched into conversation, patted the duke on the cheek, told him his young friend was most charming, and advised him to fetch her some punch. She then was claimed for a dance, and left the three.

The duke did not follow her advice. Instead, he stood like a dog guarding a bone.

"Quite a performance, old fellow," Amhearst said to his friend, clapping him on the back. "This is the liveliest I have seen this place since the waltz was introduced."

"I am afraid the beads on my slippers came loose," Betsy explained.

"Terrible," said his lordship with a shake of the head. "I hope you mean to send them back first thing tomorrow."

"I—" began Betsy.

"We are going to," said Littlefield in

strong tones, ending the subject, and again she looked at him, incensed.

"Perhaps you would care for a cup of punch," offered Lord Amhearst.

"Oh, yes. Thank you," said Betsy, smiling at him.

Amhearst left to fetch punch, and Littlefield sat down next to her. "There now," he said. "Lady Cowper herself has paid attention to you. You should feel much better."

"I do," admitted Betsy. "And I am glad someone thought to get me some punch," she added, making Littlefield feel guilty for his lack of chivalry.

"I was certainly not going to leave you with that jackanapes," he said. "Now, Elizabeth, whatever you do, don't bring up the subject of those slippers. In fact, don't talk to the fellow at all. You might encourage him."

"Would that be so bad?" countered Betsy. "He seems rather nice. And he obviously has a sense of humor."

"Ha!" snorted Littlefield. "Anyone can see humor in another man's discomfort. Why don't you shake a few beads under his feet and we shall see how hard he laughs."

Betsy's mouth twitched.

Littlefield pouted.

Lord Amhearst returned with punch for
Betsy, and she thanked him.

"It was my pleasure to serve you," said
Amhearst grandly, making Littlefield's
scowl deepen.

Littlefield caught sight of Bacon looking
their way and hailed him, determined to
introduce him to the Brightham right away
before Amhearst could distract her with
his flirting and encourage her further in
her pretensions.

Sir Harry hurried across the room. "Ah,
Littlefield, you must introduce me," he
begged.

The duke obliged, and Sir Harry
plopped onto the chair on the other side
of Betsy, launching immediately into a
long speech which at once wished her a
pleasant visit in London and catalogued
his possessions and many wonderful qualities. Betsy looked a little stunned but nodded politely and smiled.

Lord Amhearst drew his friend aside.
"Strap me, you did it! Got the chit into
Almack's just as you predicted. How you
managed it, I'll never know. The Lion will
be amazed when he hears." His lordship
stole a look at Betsy and smiled. "Taking
little thing, ain't she? Not a diamond of
the first water, grant you, but there is
something about her—something about

that smile. I cannot quite put my finger on it." Amhearst grinned. "Now, let us see if you can make a match of it between her and Bacon. I wager old Bacon will bolt before a fortnight is out."

"Why should he?" argued Littlefield. "You said yourself she ain't bad to look at. Bacon will go the distance."

"She is a nobody with no fortune," scoffed Amhearst. "The only way Bacon will offer for her is if he's foxed."

"He will offer stone cold sober," predicted Littlefield.

"In three weeks," said Amhearst.

"You are on," said the duke.

"And I shall do everything I possibly can to ensure you lose," warned Amhearst amiably.

The duke looked at Sir Harry, who was still talking at Betsy. "Try your hardest," he replied, unruffled.

Mrs. Long, seeing her granddaughter surrounded by eligible men, hurried over to meet the newest potential suitors. She beamed on Sir Harry when he asked permission to call and assured him that they would be most delighted to see him. "We are at home on Thursdays," she informed him.

"Why, tomorrow is Thursday!" exclaimed Bacon joyously.

"Why, so it is!" agreed Mrs. Long, the picture of surprise.

"I shall hope to call on you ladies tomorrow, then," said Bacon enthusiastically.

"That would be wonderful," said Mrs. Long.

Betsy said nothing.

As the duke's carriage conveyed them home later that evening, Mrs. Long was in raptures. "Only think, Betsy dearest. Two suitors already! That nice Sir Harry Bacon was positively smitten with you. He is a little portly, I admit, but such a friendly young man. And then there is Lord Amhearst. So kind of him to fetch punch for you. I do hope he is not a fortune hunter," she said to the duke. "Oh, silly me," she tittered. "Of course, he cannot be such a person if he is a friend of Your Grace's."

As if your granddaughter has any fortune to be hunted, thought Littlefield in disgust.

"No," continued Mrs. Long. "He is quite a nice young man. I can tell. All the sweet young men we have met since coming to London . . ." she rhapsodized. "It quite restores my faith in the nobility. Oh, I see a glittering season ahead of us, Betsy dear. Positively glittering! And we owe it all to our dear duke." Here she paused to look adoringly at Littlefield.

Betsy did not look adoringly at His Grace. Instead, she looked out the carriage window and sighed, and Littlefield was disappointed to find he didn't feel as satisfied with himself as he had the right to be.

Nine

There was a great curiosity among members of the ton about the young lady who had captured the attention of the Duke of Littlefield. Many of the women, having either heard Lady Jersey's account of her fateful visit to the family or talked with Mrs. Long at Almacks, were in no hurry to rush to call on them.

One woman, however, did call—a lady whom Mrs. Long pronounced as a vulgar, climbing sort of woman. "Mrs. Withersbeam, if you ask me," announced Mrs. Long as soon as their caller had left, "has heard about Lady Cowper's kindness to us. She is merely trying to find a way into Lady Cowper's good graces and sees us as a direct line. Really! What some people will not do to gain a toehold on the social ladder."

At that moment, the butler appeared to announce another visitor. "Oh, how delightful," gurgled Mrs. Long. "Now we

shall see what other important personage
wishes to further her acquaintance with
the friends of the Duke of Littlefield."

The personage who wished to further
her acquaintance turned out to be a he,
and none other than Sir Harry Bacon.

"Oh, only look who has come to call!"
declared Mrs. Long to Betsy and Mrs.
Whitworth. "It is Sir Harry. How very
good to see you again."

"The pleasure is all mine," said Sir
Harry amiably. "Wished to further my acquaintance with Miss Brightham," he announced to them all.

"It was kind of you to call," murmured
Betsy.

"You are looking very nice today," said
Sir Harry, taking her hand and bowing
over it.

"Thank you," she said.

At that moment an old woman wrapped
in several layers of shawls and wearing a
cap on her head sidled into the room and
slipped into a seat.

Mrs. Long looked mildly displeased, but
erased the look to smile at the old woman.
"Well, well, here is Betsy's great-grand-
mama. Now, Granny, dear, why don't you
go upstairs and take a nice little rest . . ."

The old woman shook her head vehe-
mently, and when Mrs. Long moved to take

her arm, pulled back against the chair. Mrs. Long frowned, then forced a smile. "Very well, then. If you wish to remain. Would you care for some tea?" The woman smiled and nodded beatifically, and looking less than beatific herself, Mrs. Long poured her mother a cup and handed it to her. "There now," she said soothingly. "You just sit here and drink your tea."

While this was going on, Sir Harry produced a snuffbox and flicked it open, helping himself.

Mrs. Long turned back to Sir Harry. "My, what a lovely snuffbox!" she declared.

Sir Harry looked pleased. "Got it just the other day," he said, passing it to her to inspect. "To add to my collection. Thus far, I have a different snuffbox for every day of the month. Petersham, himself, gave me one. It was he who started me collecting them."

"Silver filagree trim," murmured Mrs. Long.

"I am fond of silver filagree," said Bacon.

Betsy turned to see her half-brother tiptoeing into the room. "Andrew!" she reprimanded.

Mrs. Long frowned. She set the snuffbox down on the small table between her chair and her mother's, then rose and took the child by the arm. "Now, young man. You

know your sister and grandmama are entertaining visitors today and that you are not
to be anywhere near the drawing room,"
she scolded.

"I just wanted to see the fine guests,"
protested Andrew.

Sir Harry was as distracted with Andrew
as Mrs. Long and Betsy were, and didn't
see his snuffbox vanish under Granny's
shawls. "Here is a fine fellow," he said
heartily.

"This is my brother Andrew," said Betsy.
"Who is a very naughty boy," she added,
looking at Andrew levelly.

Andrew hung his head.

"Here, now. Don't scold the boy," said
Bacon amiably. "He probably ain't used to
seeing noblemen. It is a great treat for
him, I am sure."

"Oh, but I am used to seeing noblemen," the boy corrected Sir Harry, bounding to stand in front of him. "Do you
know my friend, the Duke of Littlefield?"

Bacon chuckled and looked from one
lady to the other. "I should say I do," he
said. "The duke is a friend of mine."

"Are you a Corinthian? Do you have a
fancy curricle and a coat with many capes?"

"Of course," said Bacon, and while she
smiled politely, Betsy conjured up a vision
of Littlefield in his driving coat. The im-

age of Bacon similarly attired and set next to his friend looked ridiculous, indeed.

The conversation got no further. The butler announced another caller, a woman whom Sir Harry appeared to size up and find unworthy of his time and attention, for within a few moments of her sitting down, he took his leave.

"Such a nice young man," said Mrs. Long after he was gone. "Don't you agree, Betsy dearest?"

"Yes, Grandmama," said Betsy meekly.

Littlefield called the next day to see what the Brightham thought of Sir Harry. "Oh, such a nice young man," her grandmother answered for her. "He called on us yesterday. And we had such a delightful visit!"

Littlefield grinned. "Did you?"

"We talked about his snuffbox collection," said Betsy, disgust plain in her voice.

"A great many men collect them," said Littlefield. "Why, Lord Petersham has one for every day of the year."

"How wonderful for him," murmured Betsy, and the duke frowned.

"Of course," said Mrs. Long, "Granny would insist on coming down, and for a moment I feared she might make him nervous as she did poor Lady Jersey, don't you know, but she was well behaved. And even little Andrew was a good boy and did not say anything to vex Sir Harry."

"Sir Harry Bacon," announced the butler, and ushered Sir Harry into the room.

"Sir Harry!" cried Mrs. Long as if Sir Harry were her long lost friend. "How very good to see you again."

"It is very good to see you, too, Mrs. Long," said Bacon politely. His eyes lit up at the sight of the duke. "Littlefield, old fellow! How are you?"

"Quite well," said Littlefield. "Funny you should drop by, for we were just talking of your snuffbox collection."

"Which is why I took the liberty of coming round," said Bacon. He turned to Mrs. Long. "I believe I mislaid my snuffbox here when I was visiting yesterday."

"Here?" echoed Mrs. Long.

"Yes," said Bacon. "I remember giving it to you to look at, and that was the last I saw of it. You did not find it lying on that table, perhaps?"

Mrs. Long's expression dissolved from delight to puzzlement. "Why, no," she said.

"I thought perhaps that the boy found it and thought it a pretty trinket and put it in his pocket," suggested Sir Harry.

Puzzlement changed to wide-eyed panic as the truth of who had swooped upon the pretty trinket dawned and Mrs. Long shot a nervous glance at her granddaughter, who was looking equally upset. "Oh, dear," said Mrs. Long weakly. "Oh, dear. Oh, dear."

Betsy cast a pleading look at Littlefield, who was not sure what horrible fate had befallen Bacon's snuffbox, but had his suspicions. "The servants," he said.

"Servants?" echoed Mrs. Long in surprise.

Littlefield shook his head. "I told my grandmother I thought one of her maids lightfingered." He turned to Bacon. "We shall make a thorough search of the house. That snuffbox shall be found, or a certain maid will be turned off without references, I can assure you."

Bacon frowned. "I hope it is found," he said. "I am particularly fond of that snuffbox."

"If it isn't, I know my grandmother will insist on replacing it," said Littlefield.

"Will she?" Bacon looked pleased.

"Naturally," said Littlefield firmly.

Betsy and Mrs. Long both relaxed back against the sofa cushions and a mollified Sir Harry took his leave.

"Gracious," sighed Mrs. Long after he had gone. "How you saved us!"

"Do you think the snuffbox can be recovered?" asked Littlefield.

Mrs. Long set her jaw and said, "It shall be recovered immediately."

Looking at her, the duke thought that the old bird would make a fierce opponent in a battle of wills, and hoped he never had to face her.

"If Your Grace will excuse me, I shall be back in a trice. With the snuffbox," she added, then marched from the room, looking to Littlefield like a soldier heading for battle.

"Thank you," said Betsy after she had gone, "for helping us out of a very embarrassing situation."

Littlefield smiled condescendingly at her. "Think nothing of it," he said grandly. "After all, I should hate to see you lose such a fine suitor."

The sober expression vanished from Betsy's face. "Truth to tell," she said, "I would not be so very sorry to lose Sir Harry as a suitor."

"Bacon is not such a bad sort," said Littlefield.

"He is nice enough," agreed Betsy. "But I think I like Lord Amhearst better."

"Amhearst! He is totally unsuitable for

you," protested Littlefield, seeing his wager lost.

He had barely gotten the words out of his mouth when Lord Amhearst was announced. "Littlefield!" cried his lordship, genuinely pleased to see the duke. "What are you doing here?"

"More to the point, what are you doing here?" retorted Littlefield.

"Such luck!" Mrs. Long's voice preceded her into the room. "We have found the snuffbox. Granny did, indeed—" She stopped on the threshold, the sight of Lord Amhearst cutting off her sentence. "Why, Lord Amhearst. What an honor!" She rushed into the room, curtsyed, and held out her hand to be kissed. "I am Mrs. Long. I am sure you remember meeting me at Almack's night before last. But, of course, you do, for here you are! Come to see my granddaughter, I'll wager."

"I have, as a matter of fact, come to ask Miss Brightham if she would care to go driving with me," said Amhearst.

"It is hardly the fashionable hour to go driving," said Littlefield discouragingly.

"What do Miss Brightham and I care for fashion?" replied Amhearst gaily. "Would you care to visit Kensington Gardens?"

"Oh, yes!" agreed Betsy. "I shall just

fetch my bonnet and gloves and be with
you in a trice."

Amhearst bowed and smiled.

"Oh, Betsy, dear. Why not wear your
new bonnet?" called her grandmother after her.

Under cover of her words, Littlefield
leaned over to Lord Amhearst and demanded, "What are you up to?"

"Only ensuring I win my bet," replied
his friend, and beamed at Mrs. Long, who
had turned to him, all smiles.

Betsy returned to find two very different
male countenances looking at her. Both
gentlemen rose, Lord Amhearst grinning,
the duke pouting. "I shall take my leave,"
said Littlefield stiffly, "and wish you a
good afternoon in the park."

"Thank you," said Betsy, bestowing a
chipper smile on him.

"I am sure we will enjoy it immensely,"
said Lord Amhearst, following the duke
from the room.

Littlefield snatched his hat and gloves
from the butler and marched off, making
the man scramble to get the door opened
ahead of him.

"My goodness," said Betsy.

"A poor loser," observed Amhearst.

"But what did he lose?" asked Betsy.

"Why, the pleasure of your company, of

course," replied his lordship glibly, and Betsy blushed.

Once Lord Amhearst had her settled atop his curricle, he casually asked, "And how are you enjoying your London season thus far, Miss Brightham?"

"Everyone has been so very kind to me," said Betsy. "Lady Cowper furnished vouchers to Almack's, although she had not even met me, and several people have already called on us. And, of course, the duke has been very gracious, taking us about to see the sights. Why, he even escorted us when we went shopping!"

"Such sacrifice," said Lord Amhearst.

"Oh, yes," agreed Betsy. "He was most helpful. Although it was very cruel of him to talk Grandmama out of letting me purchase that bonnet with the purple plume," she finished on a mutter.

Amhearst looked at her with interest. "Bonnet?"

She blushed. "Pray, disregard what I just said. It was most ungracious."

"Most ungracious was Littlefield's preventing a lady from having a bonnet she admired," corrected Amhearst. "Do tell me about it."

The delicate pink on Betsy's face deepened in color. "It was very silly, really," she said. "I saw a bonnet which I thought was lovely. It was quite frivolous, really. It had a large curling purple ostrich plume. I thought it would go excellently with my lilac walking gown. But the duke thought it very ugly and said I should look ridiculous in it. I am sure he was right."

"Is he always right?" asked Lord Amhearst.

"Well, in matters of dress he seems to be very knowledgeable," said Betsy.

"Oh, I am sure he is," agreed Amhearst. "He has bought enough trinkets for females these past five years."

Some of the good cheer ebbed from Betsy's face. "Oh," she said in a small voice.

Lord Amhearst seemed to realize he had spoken a little too freely. "Well, enough talk of that old spoilsport," he said heartily. "Tell me how many poor hearts you have already broken since you made your appearance among the ton Wednesday night, Miss Brightham."

Betsy blushed and smiled and obligingly turned from the subject of the Duke of Littlefield, although thoughts of him dangled about the corners of her mind—a ghost that refused to be banished. How many women had set their caps for the duke? Surely the line of contenders for his heart was a long one.

"Miss Brightham?" prompted Amhearst.

Betsy gave a start. "Oh, I am so sorry," she said. "I am afraid my mind wandered."

"Then I had best improve my conversation," said Amhearst, unoffended. "It is a sad thing when a gentleman cannot hold a lady's attention even for a short drive."

"It is a sad thing when a lady is such a rattlepate that she cannot concentrate on all the interesting things a gentleman is saying," responded Betsy politely.

"You are a very clever young woman," approved Amhearst. "Nonetheless, I shall strive to be more witty and entertaining than any man you have ever met. I shall tether your mind with my cleverness. Which would you prefer, profound statements, entertaining gossip, or silly riddles?"

Betsy clapped her hands. "Oh, silly riddles, if you please!"

"Very well," said Amhearst. "Let me think." He was silent a moment before declaring, "I have it! Answer me this if you can. Why is an ambitious clerk like a lady's bonnet," here he smiled mischievously, "a bonnet with a purple ostrich plume, in a milliner's shop?"

"Oh, gracious! I have no idea," said Betsy.

"Why, both wish to get ahead in the world," replied Amhearst, making her burst into giggles.

"How clever you are!" she declared.

Amhearst smiled, as if at some secret. "Oh, I certainly am," he said.

The duke called at his grandmother's townhouse the following day.

Mrs. Whitworth was surprised to see him. "You already paid your duty call yesterday," she said.

"It was not a duty call," said the duke stiffly. He shrugged, the picture of pretended nonchalance. "I was passing by and thought I would pop in, just to say hello."

"And to whom in particular did you wish to say hello?" pressed his grandmother.

The duke's cheeks pinkened. "Well, to you of course," he said quickly. "I thought, also, perhaps I would just ask how Elizabeth enjoyed her ride with Amhearst."

Mrs. Whitworth nodded slowly. "How very kind of you, Lionel," she said. "Ring the bell. We shall summon her. I am sure she has much to tell you."

Betsy was duly fetched and entered the room the picture of girlish excitement. "Oh, Gabriel!" she cried. "You will never guess. I have had an invitation to a rout! It came just this morning."

"Who is the hostess?" asked Littlefield.

"Mrs. Withersbeam," said Betsy, her voice still crackling with excitement.

The duke was unimpressed. "A hostess of no importance," he said.

"Well, she is important to me," said Betsy, refusing to have her enthusiasm damped. "She is the first lady who has been kind enough to invite me to a social function, and I am truly grateful." She ventured a hopeful look at the duke. "I had hoped you might escort me."

"It will be a tiresome affair and can do you no good to attend," said Littlefield.

"Lionel," chided Mrs. Whitworth.

Betsy shrugged. "Never mind," she said. "I am sure Grandmama intends to go."

Their conversation was interrupted by the arrival of a present for Betsy. She took the bandbox from the footman and sat down on the sofa with it. Discarding the lid, she pulled away the tissue paper and let out a squeal of delight, bringing out the odious hat with the purple plume. "Oh, Gabriel," she cooed.

"I did not send you that disgusting thing," protested Littlefield.

Betsy fished out the card and read it. "Why, it is from Lord Amhearst!" she declared. "Oh, how charming of him!"

"Charming? To send you such a monstrosity? It is nothing of the sort," said Littlefield. "And," he added, "it is curst improper, if you ask me."

"But no one asked you, Lionel," pointed out his grandmother.

Betsy's face lit up with inspiration. "I shall ask Lord Amhearst to escort me to the rout," she said.

"Amhearst!" cried Littlefield in disgust. "You barely know him! Why not ask old Bacon? He is already smitten with you."

"Why not Lord Amhearst?" countered Betsy.

"Never mind asking either of them," snapped Littlefield. "I shall take you myself."

"But you just said . . ."

"I am well-aware of what I just said," interrupted Littlefield. "I have changed my mind."

Betsy ran to him and hugged his arm, hanging on it and looking gratefully up at him. "Oh, you dear man. Thank you!"

"Here now," said Littlefield, embarrassed. "No need to behave like some opera dancer who has just received her first diamonds." Betsy loosened her grip and hung her head. "And I do wish you would stop calling me by that ridiculous name," he added pettishly.

This brought a teasing smile to her face.

"Very well . . . Your Grace," she added in mocking tones.

Littlefield was not amused. As he drove on to Tattersall's, he told himself the chit was a curst nuisance. Yet something rather like excitement fluttered inside his chest. He informed himself that this was merely the anticipation of finding some sport that evening and ensuring he would win his wager with Lord Amhearst. Nothing more. And to prove his point, he resolved to avoid the pesty family until the rout.

The pesty family, however, had made no such resolve where he was concerned, and Andrew showed up at the duke's townhouse the following morning just in time for breakfast. "Good morning, Your Grace," he piped, skipping past the butler. The child pulled out a chair nearest the duke and plopped onto it.

Littlefield sighed. "Good morning, Andrew," he said with resignation. "What brings you here?"

"Oh, I just came to see you and Whitey," replied Andrew casually.

"Whitey is in the cellar," said the duke.

"The cellar? Is he not very lonely in the cellar?"

"As he has chewed my Wellingtons beyond recognition, I hope he is suffering extreme pangs of loneliness. God knows he is suffering no pangs of hunger."

"Maybe he just wanted something to do," suggested Andrew.

The duke gave a snort. "He found something to do all right."

"Will he be done being punished after breakfast?" asked Andrew hopefully.

The duke smiled. The child reminded him of himself as a boy. "Yes, I suppose so," he said.

Andrew beamed, then turned his attention to his lordship's plate. "That looks very good," he observed.

"Have you not eaten breakfast?" asked Littlefield.

"Oh, yes," said Andrew. "But we did not have hot cross buns."

"Then you had best help yourself to one of mine," offered the duke.

"Oh, thank you," breathed Andrew, reaching for the duke's plate.

"On the sideboard," said Littlefield sternly.

"Yes, Your Grace," mumbled Andrew, chastised. He helped himself to a bun and returned to the table. "Betsy is very excited," he announced.

"And why, pray, is your sister excited?" asked the duke in bored accents.

"Because you are to take her to a fine

party," said Andrew. "Will you take me to a party?" he asked.

"When you are older, cub," replied the duke. "Finish your bun and we shall go throw a stick for Whitey."

When Lord Amhearst called at the Duke of Littlefield's townhouse, it was to discover His Grace playing out in back with the same little boy and mangy mongrel. "Returning to our childhood, are we?" he teased.

Littlefield was not amused. "Shut your gabblebox or you shall be returned to the dust," he warned.

Amhearst chuckled, unrepentant. "I am off to purchase Egon's second volume of *Boxiana.* I thought you might care to accompany me, but I can see you are busy."

"We were just finishing," said Littlefield firmly.

Andrew frowned, and the duke rumpled his curls. "Here now, cub. I have other things to do today besides play with this wretched cur. You may remain. Have a footman escort you home when you have worn out the mongrel."

"Yes, Your Grace," said Andrew in resigned tones.

"So," said Amhearst, a little later, "you take the entire family under your wing, do you?"

"I certainly do not!" snapped Littlefield. "People will talk."

"People may go to the devil!" replied the duke.

"This sounds like a man in love," observed Amhearst.

"And you sound like a man who has taken leave of his senses," retorted Littlefield. "I am heartily sick of the subject of that curst female and her curst family, and unless you want me to plant you a facer, you will drop it immediately."

Lord Amhearst remained unruffled. "But of course," he said. "She is a taking little thing," he added after a moment.

"Amhearst," said Littlefield in warning tones.

Lord Amhearst merely laughed and changed the subject.

But Littlefield felt as if he had Miss Elizabeth Brightham perched on his shoulder the rest of the day, and no amount of Bond Street lounging could shake her off. He returned home in a very sour mood and immediately went to the dining room to fetch a bottle of wine from the sideboard. He poured himself a glass and tossed it off. "Curst chit," he muttered. "Curst family. Curst nuisance!" He kicked the sideboard, making the china in it rattle, then, feeling

no better, limped off to his library to stare
at the book lined shelves and brood.

Betsy entered Mrs. Withersbeam's townhouse, her face a picture of excitement.
"Oh, my," she said to the duke. "What a
grand assembly."

"Oh, yes," agreed her grandmama.

The duke scanned the room. Their fellow guests seemed nothing much to him,
although he noticed that Lord Amhearst
and the Flower were present, along with
their mother, Lady Amhearst. There was
the Lion smiling at him in a very annoying
way, and he wondered if Amhearst had
been spreading tales. The duke frowned,
then caught sight of Sir Harry Bacon.

Ah, very good! The sport would continue.

Sir Harry Bacon looked their way. Littlefield hailed him, and Sir Harry hurried
over. "Ah, Miss Brightham," he said, taking in Betsy's flounced satin gown, "you
are looking exceptionally lovely tonight."

"I told her that rose color would suit
her," said the duke.

"Oh, most definitely," agreed Bacon.
"You should listen to the duke. He has
excellent taste."

"Oh, yes," parroted Mrs. Long, who was

standing on the other side of the duke. "Excellent taste."

"It is a pity she does not allow my taste to guide her in the matter of bonnets," said Littlefield.

Betsy, instead of looking penitent, raised her fan to cover a mischievous smile.

"Ah, well," said the duke, "There you have it."

"Er, yes," said Bacon, bewildered.

Littlefield turned to Betsy. "Would you care for some punch?"

"None for me, my dear boy," put in Mrs. Long. "I see Lady Albert, and I must go and say hello to her. We met at Almack's, and I wish to renew the acquaintance."

With that, she hurried off, and the duke heaved a sigh of relief and turned again to Betsy.

"I would like some punch," she said. "I must confess, I am nervous, and my throat is very dry."

"No need to be nervous," whispered the duke, patting her arm reassuringly. "There is no one here worthy of causing it." In a normal tone, he continued, "I see a footman with a tray of cups. I shall waylay him if Sir Harry will be good enough to bear you company."

"Of course," said Bacon, smiling at Betsy. "Would you care to sit, Miss Brightham?"

Betsy thought that an excellent idea, for her legs were definitely feeling a little weak. These people did not frighten the duke. He was accustomed to moving in such circles. But they made her very nervous.

Before Littlefield could return, Lord Amhearst came to greet her, taking a seat on the other side of her. Sir Harry greeted his rival with an underwhelming show of enthusiasm. "Amhearst. Good to see you. It would appear your sister is looking a little at sea. Perhaps you had best return to her."

"Oh, not before I have had a chance to thank Lord Amhearst for his kind gift," protested Betsy. She smiled at Amhearst. "It was terribly sweet of you."

Amhearst grinned. "Now you have your purple-plumed bonnet to match your lilac walking dress. And I hope you will allow me to take you walking in Hyde Park. We shall test the effect of the ensemble on the ton."

"I am sure every lady will envy me my fetching bonnet," said Betsy.

"I am sure they will," agreed Lord Amhearst.

At that moment, the duke returned. "The Flower looks lost," he informed his friend. "Perhaps you had best go rescue her."

Amhearst grimaced. "Duty calls," he said to Betsy, and left them.

"Pesty fellow," muttered Bacon. "Now, where were we?"

"Telling Miss Brightham how lovely she looked," the duke reminded him.

"Oh, yes, of course."

"Who is that girl?" Lady Hyacinth asked her brother.

Lord Amhearst followed her gaze to Betsy. "No one in particular," he said. "Hyacinth, have you greeted Miss Bostrom yet? I see her over there in the corner with her mama." And with that, he steered his sister to the end of the room farthest from Betsy.

But Betsy had seen Lady Hyacinth looking at her. "Who is that with Lord Amhearst?" she asked the duke.

"The Flower? It is his little sister. She is making her come-out this season, same as you."

"Truly! She looks a very sweet creature. I should like to meet her."

"Now?" protested Littlefield. "But Sir Harry . . ."

"Oh, I am sure Sir Harry will excuse us

for a moment. Poor Sir Harry, most likely, has many people to talk to, and it would be unfair to burden him with my company all night long."

"No burden, I assure you," said Bacon earnestly.

"You are too kind, sir," said Betsy. "Will you excuse us?"

"Certainly," said Bacon, disappointed.

"You have discouraged him," said Littlefield as he led her off.

"And that displeases you?" asked Betsy.

"Well, it is hardly a matter of what pleases and displeases me," stuttered Littlefield. "You are the one who has come to London to make a great match."

"I was *brought* to London to make a great match," corrected Betsy.

"That is what I just said," said Littlefield irritably.

Betsy merely shook her head and looked at him as if he were obtuse.

It irritated him greatly, and his displeasure showed in the curt introduction he made to Lady Hyacinth.

Neither girl seemed to notice. "This is my first rout," confessed Betsy, taking a seat next to Lady Hyacinth.

"It is mine, also," said the girl. "It is not half so frightening as a come-out ball, though," she added, "I have had mine. Have you had yours?"

Betsy bit her lip, feeling embarrassed that she had not yet had such an affair. She wasn't at all sure she would. At any rate, who would come? So few people knew her. "I have not," she said.

Lady Hyacinth looked unsure how to reply to this, so she merely said, "Oh."

Mrs. Long descended on them, staying long enough to gush over Lady Hyacinth and invite her and her mama to call on them, then towing Betsy off to say hello to Lady Albert.

Littlefield remained with Lady Hyacinth until her brother returned, then after informing his friend that all the bonnets in the world would not win him his wager, took himself off.

"What a very odd remark," observed Lady Hyacinth. "What did it mean?"

"Nothing, love," said her brother. "Never mind Littlefield. What were you doing talking with Miss Brightham?"

"The duke introduced us. I liked her."

"Well, don't go thinking to become bosom bows," advised Amhearst. "The girl can do you no good."

"What do you mean, Tony?"

Lord Amhearst obviously did not wish to be pressed. He seemed uncomfortable searching for the right words. "Miss Brightham is a nobody. It is a nine day's wonder she got vouchers to Almack's. She will, most likely, end up as someone's . . . well, never mind."

"Mistress?" gasped Lady Hyacinth.

Amhearst scowled. "Hyacinth," he began.

"But whose mistress?" she persisted.

Her brother's cheeks turned red. "Never you mind," he snapped. "And don't let me hear you talking of such things. It ain't ladylike."

Lady Hyacinth regarded Betsy thoughtfully. "But she did get into Almack's. She must be ton."

"Not really," said Amhearst. "She has no connections and no money, and she will disappear before the season is even over."

"But she must have some connections," protested his sister. "She is here with the Duke of Littlefield."

"It is a very slender connection, dearest, I assure you," said Amhearst. "Littlefield means to be shed of her as soon as possible, one way or another."

"Oh," said his sister, digesting this interesting information. "I wonder if she knows," she mused.

"Good God, no!" exclaimed her brother. "And you ain't to tell her. In fact, it really would be best if you did not speak to her again if you should see her."

"Cut her?" Hyacinth looked shocked.

"She can do you no good," repeated Amhearst. Lady Hyacinth did not look inclined to agree. "Hyacinth," he said sternly. "You must promise not to befriend her."

"I promise," said Lady Hyacinth, hiding her slender gloved hand in the folds of her skirt and crossing her fingers.

Ten

Lady Hyacinth finally convinced her mama it would be in their best interests to pay a call on the family that was making their social debut under the wing of the Duke of Littlefield. As the duke's grandmama, with whom they stayed, was not ton, this took some doing. But at last her ladyship gave in.

As the butler ushered them in, Lady Amhearst took in the entrance hall, decorated only with a table and mirror near the stairs and another small table with a marble bust alongside the wall, and saw evidence of good taste. Mrs. Whitworth's drawing room was elegant but not ostentatious. A slightly worn Aubusson carpet cushioned her ladyship's feet as she walked into the room. The heavy red velvet drapes, she noticed, while not worn, were hardly new. Mrs. Whitworth was not one to flaunt her wealth. Unconsciously, Lady Amhearst nodded her head in approval.

If Mrs. Whitworth noticed this, she gave no indication of it, other than a faint smile, and bid her callers welcome.

Mrs. Long, who, along with Betsy, was bearing her company, was not quite so restrained. "Oh, how wonderful!" she gushed. "Only look who has come to see us, Betsy dear."

"Yes, Grandmama, I see," replied Betsy calmly, and smiled at Lady Hyacinth. "I am happy to see you again," she said to the girl. "Would you care to come sit next to me on the sofa?"

Lady Hyacinth was delighted to do so. Her mama took a seat with less delight. "What a lovely, lovely gown you are wearing!" exclaimed Betsy.

Lady Hyacinth beamed. "Do you like it, really?"

"Oh, yes," said Betsy. "And I especially like the bonnet you are wearing with it. I am quite fond of plumes," she confessed. "I saw a lovely one when the duke accompanied us shopping, but he made such a fuss Grandmama would not let me have it." She smiled, forcing out a dimple. "But your brother bought it for me and made me a gift of it."

"Oh, my," said Lady Hyacinth, impressed. "My brother did that for you?"

Betsy nodded. "He is a very kind gentleman." Lady Hyacinth bit her lip, troubled, but Betsy did not notice. "Next time the duke takes me out driving, I intend to wear it to tease him."

"The duke does not . . . make you nervous?" ventured Lady Hyacinth.

"Gracious, no," said Betsy. "Does he you?"

"Oh, yes," said the girl. "I am sure he does not mean to. He has always treated me just like a little sister." She looked down at her gloved hands lying in her lap. "I suppose that is why he makes me nervous. I always feel that he is about to pull my curls or remind me of something silly I did when I was little."

Mrs. Long had been managing to keep track of two conversations at once and now inserted herself into Betsy and Lady Hyacinth's. "Our dear duke is such a tease," she said. "But you must not mind him. In fact, you must always say exactly what you think to him, for I believe he appreciates that. Don't you, Betsy dearest?"

Betsy felt Lady Amhearst's disapproving gaze on her and felt her face grow warm. "I am sure I would not presume to say what the duke would or would not like," she said in a small voice.

"Very proper," approved Lady Amhearst, and the look she gave Mrs. Long told that good woman that she might learn something from her granddaughter.

Both young ladies fell into an intimidated silence, and the conversation limped along for another ten minutes before Lady Amhearst said, "Well now, Hyacinth, I think we should be on our way. We have other calls to make. So nice to have met you," she said condescendingly to Mrs. Whitworth, who inclined her head.

Lady Hyacinth rose. "We are at home on Tuesdays," she told Betsy. "I hope you will call on us."

Her mama looked none too pleased by this invitation but managed a smile. "I am sure Mrs. Long has many social obligations," said her ladyship. "You mustn't press her."

Lady Hyacinth opened her mouth to protest but got no opportunity, for her ladyship was quickly bidding everyone farewell and making for the door. The girl said a hasty goodbye and hurried after her mama.

"Well, now," said Mrs. Long after the guests had been shown out, "there is a nice new friend for you, Betsy dear."

Betsy smiled. "I like her," she said.

Mrs. Whitworth said nothing.

The following Tuesday, Mrs. Long took

Betsy to call upon Lady Amhearst and her daughter.

Lady Amhearst looked anything but pleased to see Mrs. Long, and the woman who was visiting with her stayed only long enough to bid the newcomers a stiff hello followed by a stiff goodbye, then took herself off.

"Well, now," said Mrs. Long, falling onto a chair. "I should have thought your ladyship's drawing room to be chock-full of callers at this time of day. Ah, well. We shall have a comfortable coze, just the four of us." And here she beamed on the two girls.

Unaware of her mother's lack of enthusiasm for their callers, Lady Hyacinth plunged into conversation with Betsy. "When is your come-out ball to be held?"

Betsy wasn't sure and hesitated over her answer, and her grandmother stepped into the breach. "Why, within the next fortnight, I am sure. It is going to be held at Littlefield House, don't you know."

"My," breathed Lady Hyacinth, impressed.

"I imagine you and your mama should be getting your invitation any day now," continued Mrs. Long.

"And how is it you are acquainted with

the duke?" asked Lady Amhearst, politely probing.

"Oh, the duke's grandmama and I are old friends. We attended Miss Marrywell's Seminary for Young Ladies together when we were girls. Now, if that ain't a long-standing friendship, I don't know what is."

Lady Amhearst gave the faintest nod politeness would allow.

Mrs. Long smiled determinedly. "I imagine your pretty daughter had a lovely come-out ball," she said.

"It was," agreed her ladyship. She looked to the clock on the mantle. "My, look at the time! I am sure you have many more calls to make."

"Oh, I think we might stay another few minutes," said Mrs. Long.

"Grandmama," said Betsy, "I am afraid I am not feeling quite well. Perhaps we should be on our way."

"Oh, my. We cannot have you falling ill," said her grandmother. "Life moves at such a fast pace in the city," she informed Lady Amhearst. "Well, then. We shall be off." She rose and Betsy followed suit. "So nice to have seen your ladyship."

"Thank you for calling," said Lady Amhearst in tones which showed a distinct lack of thanks. Their unwelcome guests were shown out, and she heaved a sigh.

"Such a creature! I do wonder what they hold over Littlefield. Well, that is what comes of marrying below one's station. One must forever be contending with such embarrassing connections."

"But the duke is not married," said Lady Hyacinth, confused.

"I was speaking of the duke's father. And a very foolish match it was, too. He married a girl much beneath him. And you can see how long lasting are the results of such a mistake, my dear. Take it very much to heart."

Lady Hyacinth bit her lip. At last she said, "But we may attend the ball, mayn't we? If it is to be held at the duke's townhouse?"

"If it is held at the duke's townhouse, I shall eat my slippers," said her ladyship skeptically.

"But if it is?" persisted Lady Hyacinth.

"We shall see," said Lady Amhearst noncommittally.

"Such a woman!" declared Mrs. Long once they were safely inside her friend's carriage. "I never saw such rudeness. I have always said, there is nothing noble about the nobility, and here you have proof. They are all selfish and proud."

"The Duke of Littlefield is not like that," said Betsy.

"True, true," agreed her grandmother.

"Funny," Betsy mused. "I thought he was when we first met him. But he is not at all what I first supposed him to be."

Her grandmother studied her, and she blushed under the scrutiny. "Don't look too high, child," she cautioned. "Remember to be sensible and take the first reasonable offer you get. You hold out for the moon and you may wind up with naught but a fistful of moonbeams."

Betsy sighed. "Yes, Grandmama," she said. "I suppose you are right. But does it not seem that the duke spends a great deal of time—"

"He spends a great deal of time because it pleases him to please his grandmama, who holds the purse strings," said Mrs. Long. "Don't delude yourself, child, into thinking he pays attention to you for any other reason."

"Grandmama!" cried Betsy, shocked. "Here you are always calling him 'our dear duke,' and fawning over him as if he were a knight sprung from the pages of a book."

"And so he is our dear duke. We may be very glad he dances so well to his grandmother's piping, and we may be glad his grandmother and I are friends, for it has provided you with an entrance to society which I could not. Though why I should want to put you into such a society I cannot imagine," mused the old woman.

"Because Mama would have wanted it?" prompted Betsy gently, and her grandmama nodded and squeezed her hand.

"And I know you will do your mama proud and not choose as foolishly as she once did. That nice Sir Harry would make you a fine husband."

"Grandmama!" chided Betsy.

"Oh, I know he ain't much to behold," said Mrs. Long. "But that is why I know he will make a good husband. Judging from his looks, I should say he thinks more of the dinner table than the gambling table, and that, considering your poor mama's misfortune, is a true blessing."

"I had rather marry for love," said Betsy.

"Your mama married for love," pointed out Mrs. Long.

"Well, then, if not for love, at least to someone I may like and respect."

"And who might that be?" asked Mrs. Long suspiciously. "Other than the duke."

Betsy shrugged. "I don't know," she said, suddenly listless. "Perhaps Lord Amhearst."

"He seems a nice enough young man,"

conceded Mrs. Long. "But don't let your hopes fly too high in that direction, for I fear his mama would rather see him remain a bachelor all his days than be linked with us."

It was now Betsy's turn to sigh. "Perhaps we had best return home," she said. "I shall marry Tommy Walker and be done with it."

"A bootmaker? My dear child, your mother would turn in her grave." Betsy sighed, and her grandmother patted her hand. "Now, don't despair. Your season has barely begun, and your come-out is being sponsored by the Duke of Littlefield. It cannot help but be successful. Once the likes of Lady Amhearst attend your come-out ball at the duke's townhouse, they will all sing another tune."

"Oh, dear," fretted Betsy. "We have not even set a date for this ball, and you have already told Lady Amhearst of it. What if the duke has decided he does not wish to give us the use of his house?"

Mrs. Long smiled slyly. "I should say it is now a little too late for that."

Summons from his grandmother were now commonplace, and the duke went like the tame animal he was becoming. He bent to kiss his grandmama's cheek and asked her if more silverware was missing. "Don't tease me, Lionel. I am not in the mood," she snapped. "I sent for you because we must set a date for this come-out ball. Betsy and her grandmama have paid a call on Lady Amhearst, and from what I can gather, her ladyship expects an invitation any day."

"You have the use of Littlefield House. Only set the date," said the duke easily.

"Well, what day do you have free within the next fortnight?"

"I?"

"Yes, you," said Mrs. Whitworth irritably.

"What does it matter when I am free?"

"Because your presence is required."

"I am not the host of this thing."

"You most certainly are," said his grandmother. "What good will it do to have a ball at your house if you aren't there to lend it countenance?"

"Having the thing at my house should lend it countenance enough," declared Littlefield. "Besides, I ain't married. Who would act my hostess?"

"I am sure you will have no trouble finding a hostess," said Mrs. Whitworth. "Perhaps your paternal grandmother?"

"And how, pray, am I to persuade her

to host a ball for some pretentious little nobody she has never met?"

"You are a clever boy. You will think of something. Once she meets Betsy, she may decide she wishes to help the girl."

"To know her is to love her," said the duke.

"Such snide remarks do not become you, Lionel," said his grandmama.

Littlefield knew it had been a cruel thing to say, and it made him all the more snappish. "Well, what do you suggest I do?" he demanded.

"You have said it yourself. To know her is to love her. Can you not take her to call on your grandmother?"

Littlefield sighed heavily. "I shall think of something," he promised.

"I suggest you think quickly," said his grandmother.

The duke took his leave and went to Brooks's to mull over this latest problem. Well, every sport had its challenge. In boxing, it was how to get in a hit over the other man's guard. In hunting, it was how to take the fences and keep your seat. In bringing out Betsy, it was how to get the chit properly accepted by polite society—and how to find a proper hostess to help him.

"Why so glum?" came a voice from the wing chair opposite his.

Littlefield looked up to see Lord Amhearst fall into a chair across from him, a teasing smile tugging at the corners of his mouth. "I have to find a hostess for the Brightham's come-out ball," said Littlefield.

Lord Amhearst shook his head. "Hopeless," he said. "Best concede your wager here and now. The girl's family is a ball and chain dragging her down. She'll never take. Even Bacon is bound to see that before three weeks is over."

Littlefield scowled. "She'll take," he vowed.

"She'll end up someone's bit of muslin," predicted Amhearst.

"Take a powder," said Littlefield in disgust.

His friend shrugged. "Touchy, ain't you, about a little nobody?"

"I ain't touchy," retorted the duke. "And if you think I cannot rise to a challenge, you are very much mistaken." He fell back into thoughtful silence, searching the jumble of names and faces swimming in his brain. "I have it!" he declared, snapping his fingers. "Maddy!"

"Your cousin?"

Littlefield nodded. "She's quite the society hostess these days."

"Which is why she won't want to ruin her reputation with some nobody."

Littlefield jutted his chin out to a pugnacious angle. "Which is why she'll rise to a challenge," he predicted.

"Perhaps," said Amhearst nonchalantly.

The duke didn't remain to hear any more of his friend's doubts and aspersions. He strode with great energy from the room, anxious to fetch Betsy and pay a call immediately on his cousin, Lady Browning.

The duke arrived at Mrs. Whitworth's townhouse like a general descending on his troops. "I want Miss Brightham down here in her best gown and ready to pay a social call in twenty minutes," he informed the butler. "Where is my grandmother?"

"She is resting, Your Grace," said the man. "I believe Mrs. Long is up."

"Well, don't tell her I am here, for God's sake," snapped the duke. "I shall wait in the library."

Half an hour later, Betsy entered the library, wearing her lilac walking gown and the monstrous hat with the purple plume that Littlefield despised. He frowned. "Must you wear that bonnet?" he complained.

"I am fond of this bonnet," said Betsy.

"And I am sure, although Your Grace would wish to command me in what bonnet I wear, as he does in all else, I prefer to retain some small amount of freedom."

Littlefield frowned. The girl was going to be difficult. Well, no sense making a scene. He had seen his cousin in bonnets equally atrocious. "Very well," he said. "Let us be off."

"Might I enquire where we are bound?" asked Betsy sweetly.

"We are going to visit my cousin, Lady Browning. I wish to ask her to act as hostess at your come-out ball, and I think she might want to meet you before committing herself."

"So I am to be inspected, like an ell of cloth," said Betsy.

"One is always being inspected every time one meets new people," pointed out the duke.

She sighed. "I suppose you are right," she said.

She looked almost dejected, thought Littlefield. Ladies weren't supposed to look dejected when they went calling. It was what they liked to do most. In an effort to perk her up, he said, "You will like my cousin. Maddy was always up for a little fun and gig. Slap up to the nines."

"I am sure she is wonderful," said Betsy obligingly.

As they drove to Lady Browning's, the duke again attempted to revive his normally cheery companion's spirits. "I guess that bonnet ain't so bad," he offered.

"I am glad it now has your approval," she said.

Littlefield looked at her, exasperated. "I don't know why you are being so curst difficult today," he complained.

"You are right," she said.

"Well, I wish you might stop it. We will never get Maddy to sponsor you if you keep up this odd start."

"Then you would be free of your obligation to help me," said Betsy. "You could truly say you did all you possibly could."

The duke stopped his curricle in front of his cousin's house. "This is a ridiculous conversation," he observed. He hopped down from the curricle and fairly jerked Betsy down after him. Leaving his tiger to walk the horses, he escorted her up the walk to the Browning's townhouse at a very brisk pace, his lips clamped together tightly.

Betsy kept pace with him, her lips equally tight, and when Lady Browning's butler opened the door, it was to a couple who looked more as if they had come to do violence to Lady Browning than to pay a social call. "Good day, Your Grace," said the butler, swinging wide the door.

"Good day," snapped Littlefield. "I have come to see Lady Browning."

"Yes, Your Grace," murmured the butler, and ushered the pair into a drawing room of luxurious velvets and satins in colors of cream and pink.

Her ladyship, a lovely woman with rich dark curls and large brown eyes, reclined on a sofa of pink-striped brocade. Her eyes brightened at the sight of the duke. "Lionel!" she cried. "I am so glad you are come. I am heartily bored!" She stole a look at Betsy. "Is this the young lady who made you trip on the dance floor at Almack's? I have heard all about it and I am heartily sick that I missed it." She ignored her cousin's frown and turned her smile full on Betsy, who smiled back.

It was the first smile Littlefield had seen since he called for the girl, and he took it as a sign of hope. "This is Lady Browning," he said.

"It is a pleasure to meet you at last," said Lady Browning. "I am sorry I have not called to pay my respects. Life has been such a whirl these past two weeks, I have barely had time to breathe."

"That is quite all right," said Betsy politely. "It is nice to meet you."

"Do sit," said her ladyship. "I shall ring for tea and cakes and we will have a cozy chat."

"That would be a relief," said Betsy, perching on a chair.

Lady Browning raised her eyebrows inquisitively.

Betsy colored a little, lifted her chin, and said, "I should certainly prefer it to being inspected like a horse for sale."

Lady Browning giggled and the duke frowned. "I should think so," said her ladyship. "And is that why you think you were brought here?"

"I really could not say, your ladyship," replied Betsy. "I can only surmise."

Something like a growl could be heard from Littlefield's corner of the room, and Lady Browning smiled. "I suppose you have been bullying this poor creature around something fierce," she said.

"I certainly have not," protested the duke. "I've merely been trying to show her the ropes."

"I see," said Lady Browning in a superior way which made Littlefield itch to turn her over his knee.

"Actually, His Grace has been most kind to me and my family," said Betsy, now re-pentant of her earlier words. "He procured vouchers to Almack's for us, and he has taken us to Vauxhall, and, of course—"

Lady Browning held up a dainty white hand. "Oh, pray, say no more. I am already quite fatigued with hearing of all the good deeds which my noble cousin has done. I can assure you, it is quite out of character."

Littlefield suddenly wondered what ever had possessed him to praise his devilish cousin so highly.

Refreshments arrived. The ladies took to discussing fashion, and the duke let his mind wander. Maddy had always been a favorite cousin. They had played together as children, and he was godfather to her son. He watched the two women talking and thought how well they got along. It was clear they had hit it off, and that meant Maddy would gladly act as hostess for Elizabeth.

The duke grinned. Ha! Here was one wager poor old Amhearst was bound to lose. That *was* all it was to Amhearst, wasn't it? A wager? Could he possibly have designs on Elizabeth? If so, they weren't honorable, damn his eyes! Littlefield frowned.

"Lionel, do you not care for your seed cake?" asked his cousin.

"What? Oh, yes. Very good. Well, Elizabeth, if you are finished, I suppose I should take you home."

"Certainly," said the girl obligingly. Quite a difference from the termagant he had driven over here, he thought. Well, a man must keep a tight rein, never let them have their heads. She knows who is in charge now.

"And how did you like my cousin?" he asked as they trotted through the streets of Mayfair.

"I thought her quite nice," said Betsy.

"Good," said the duke. "For I intend to ask her to act as hostess for your come-out ball."

"Oh, how nice that would be!" declared Betsy. "I should not feel at all nervous if Lady Browning were there by my side." She smiled at the duke. "That was really most thoughtful of you, Gabriel," she said.

"Elizabeth," he began sternly.

"Oh, please don't scold me," she said, laying a hand on his arm.

For some ridiculous reason, he found the touch very pleasing. Well, of course, you do, saphead! he scolded himself. You are a male and she is a female. A new mistress is what you need.

"It is only that, well, I don't care what my grandmother may say . . ."

"What? What does your grandmother

say?" he asked, trying to pick up the threads of the lost conversation.

Betsy blushed. "It is of no consequence," she said. "I really am very grateful to you for all you have done for me."

"I am enjoying it," he said, as if daring her to tell him he weren't. "It is a challenge."

"A challenge," she said thoughtfully. "Ah, yes. I can see how it would be."

She was oddly silent the rest of the way home, and the duke regretted his words, wishing he could take them back. "Elizabeth," he said when they reached her doorstep, "I did not mean . . ."

"I know," she said brightly, her eyes glistening. "Thank you very much for a lovely afternoon." And with that the door was opened, and she was gone, hurrying up the stairs, and the duke was left feeling less than satisfied with the way the afternoon had come off.

Instead of going home, he hurried back to his cousin's, sure that to know success in his venture would wipe away the odd and indescribable feeling chewing at his heart.

"I thought you might be back," crowed Lady Browning.

"Well, and what do you think of her?" he asked anxiously.

"Why, that she was perfectly charming and would make you an excellent wife."

"What!" stammered Littlefield.

"Are you not grooming her to be your duchess?" asked Lady Browning innocently.

"Are you mad? She is a toad-eating little nobody from nowhere without a penny to her name."

"Then why are you giving her entree into the ton?" enquired his cousin.

"Because Grandmother wishes it," roared Littlefield.

Lady Browning was not intimidated. "Our grandmother? Or your grandmother?"

Littlefield grimaced. "Which do you think?" he countered.

"And why did you bring this little nobody to meet me?" asked Lady Browning, leaning back against the sofa cushions and regarding him.

"Because I have been coerced into offering Littlefield House for her come-out ball and I need a hostess."

Lady Browning snickered. "I see your grandmother is leading you a merry dance this season."

Littlefield shrugged. "I am making it one," he said mysteriously. "And I wish her to take."

"So I have heard," said her ladyship.

Littlefield looked questioningly at her.

"My husband heard of your little wager with Lord Amhearst. Are we to spread it about at her ball that she is a great heiress? And while we are at it, we might find her a relation who is nobility. Perhaps we can claim some distant relationship with the Prince Regent."

Littlefield blushed under his cousin's scathing gaze. "Now, Maddy, you quite misunderstand," he began.

"I understand perfectly," said his cousin lightly. "It was an odious, beastly thing to do, Lionel, and I shall be happy to act as your hostess, for I intend to do everything I possibly can to ensure Miss Brightham's social success. I already have several wonderful dance partners in mind for her."

"Here now, Maddy. There is no reason to fly up into the boughs," protested Littlefield.

"I have set the date already," Lady Browning continued. "We have only Miss Manchester's come-out and Lady Dalton's musicale with which to compete. I assume you are giving me *carte blanche* as to refreshments and decorations. A running supper, I believe, will be nice. And ices from Gunther's, naturally."

"Naturally," agreed the duke irritably, feeling that, like Cain, his punishment was going to be far greater than his crime.

"I shall call on Miss Brightham tomorrow, and we will begin preparations immediately," announced Lady Browning. "Now, run along, Lionel. I have much to do."

Run along? Maddy was telling the Duke of Littlefield to run along? For a moment he stared at her, hardly believing his ears. She paid him no mind, rising from her sofa and heading for the drawing-room door. Scowling, he followed her out. "Just see that you don't spend every last farthing I own," he grumped. "I ain't Midas, you know."

The following day Lady Browning called on Betsy and met her family. She refused to be irritated by Mrs. Long's toadying or shocked by the crone who drifted about the drawing room, fingering Mrs. Whitworth's diminishing supply of trinkets. Instead, like all good generals, she kept her mind on the campaign ahead. "We have much to do," she said. "Today, we shall go to the printer's and see about invitations. Mrs. Long, I think, perhaps you and Mrs. Whitworth might not mind so very much addressing invitations? Tomorrow Miss Brightham and I will pay some social calls. Later this week I shall order the greens. I think, perhaps, potted palms. And, I think, a little fountain at one end of the ballroom would be charming. Don't you?"

"Oh, my," said Betsy. "It all sounds rather costly."

Lady Browning smiled wickedly. "Oh, it will be, I assure you," she said.

The duke called at his grandmother's house several times the following week, but never found Miss Brightham home. One day she was out paying social calls with Lady Browning; the next she was off at the Pavillion, searching for Chinese lanterns and fans. The third time Littlefield called, Elizabeth was at Lady Browning's dress-maker, being fitted for a ballgown. "There was nothing wrong with the ballgowns *I* chose for her," he complained to his grand-mother.

"Lady Browning has impeccable taste," said his grandmother.

"*I* have impeccable taste as well," asserted Littlefield, perturbed.

"Of course you do, Lionel," said his grandmother soothingly. "And the ball-gowns you chose for her were very nice."

"Then why the devil is she racketing about town purchasing more—when she has not even worn all the ones we chose—instead of staying home to receive visi-tors?" exploded Littlefield.

"Lionel. You must not feel put out that

you are no longer needed," said Mrs. Whitworth soothingly.

"Put out? No longer needed?" Littlefield waved the ridiculous words away. "Bah! I have things to do."

"I am sure you do, dear," said his grandmama calmly. "Run along now and do them, and I shall tell Betsy you called."

"You may tell her," said the duke stiffly, "that I am afraid this is the last time I will be able to call on her before the ball. I shall look forward to seeing you then."

"Very well," said his grandmother, unperturbed, and offered her cheek to be kissed.

The duke made his exit and went directly to Jackson's, feeling a sudden need for fisticuffs.

Eleven

As the duke was making his way to Jackson's boxing saloon, Betsy was finishing up her fitting session at the dressmaker's. Lady Browning, while waiting for her, had been looking at fashion plates, toying with the idea of ordering a new gown herself. Two ladies entered the shop, and her ladyship looked up to see Lady Amhearst and her daughter. "Lady Amhearst," she said genially. "It is so very good to see you."

Lady Amhearst greeted the young matron cordially, for Lady Browning was an up-and-coming hostess. Her balls and fêtes were famous for their mix of interesting and important people.

"Is your lovely daughter here to collect a gown to wear to my protégée's come-out ball?" asked Lady Browning. At that moment, her protégée stepped out of the fitting room.

"Miss Brightham," managed Lady Amhearst. She turned amazed eyes to Lady Browning.

"Have you met Miss Brightham?" asked Lady Browning.

"Why, yes, we have," said Lady Amhearst, amazement still plain in her voice.

"I do hope you are planning to give us the pleasure of your company at her come-out ball next week," said Lady Browning. "I assure you, Littlefield House will rival Vauxhall by the time we are done decorating. It will be a sight you shan't wish to miss."

"I am sure," agreed Lady Amhearst, her voice unsure.

"It sounds lovely," put in Lady Hyacinth, smiling at her friend.

Lady Browning beamed approvingly at her, then turned to Betsy. "I suppose we should be off, dearest," she said. "We still have much to do today." Bidding Lady Amhearst and her daughter farewell, Lady Browning left her to stand in the reception room gaping, her daughter smiling in anticipation.

The ladies finally returned home to find Sir Harry in the drawing room, enduring Mrs. Long's company. His face brightened at the sight of Betsy, and he came and bowed over her hand. "Ah, Miss Brightham! I was about to give up and

Now I am glad I did not. I understand you are very busy preparing for your upcoming ball. I came to beg you to save me a waltz."

"I am afraid Miss Brightham has already promised every dance," said Lady Browning dampingly.

Sir Harry looked crestfallen. Mrs. Long frowned. "Such a naughty habit this is becoming! Young ladies promising gentlemen dances before the ball has even begun." She turned smilingly to Sir Harry. "I am sure Betsy will be able to find room for you, Sir Harry."

Bacon beamed at this and, after a few more minutes, took his leave.

As soon as he was gone, Mrs. Long turned to Lady Browning. "We really mustn't discourage Sir Harry. He is Betsy's most ardent suitor, don't you know."

"We can do better than Sir Harry," said her ladyship confidently. "I assure you, before this ball is over, you will be the talk of London," she told Betsy.

Betsy wasn't sure she wanted to be the talk of London, but she kept her doubts to herself and merely thanked Lady Browning for all she was doing. Really, all she wanted was . . . She clamped the lid firmly down on that thought. There was no sense dreaming of what was impossible.

* * *

The day of the ball arrived and Betsy sat before her dressing table draped in a satin slip dress the color of champagne with a gold net over it. She looked at the posy of small, cream-colored roses from Lord Amhearst, and the gardenia from Sir Harry, which her abigail was about to pin in her hair, and sighed.

A knock at her door heralded the arrival of Mrs. Long, an awesome sight in a puce-colored evening gown and a matching turban. "Oh, my dear, you look breathtakingly lovely!" she exclaimed.

Little Andrew scampered in behind her. "You look like a fairy princess!" he declared. He went to her dressing table and picked up the posy of roses, burying his nose in them. "These smell good," he announced.

Betsy merely sighed.

"Flowers from two gentlemen," raved Mrs. Long. "I declare, such a fortunate young woman you are!"

"There has been nothing delivered from the duke?" asked Betsy.

Mrs. Long frowned. "He has given us the use of his townhouse, child."

Betsy's shoulders drooped despondently. "I know, Grandmama," she murmured.

"Come now, my dear. I know many a young lady who would give anything for the two suitors you have."

"You are right, of course," agreed Betsy.

"When can I go to a ball?" asked Andrew.

"When you are a grown man," said his grandmother. "And now you must go to bed."

Another knock sounded on Betsy's door, and her maid went to answer it. The distraction made Mrs. Long forget to send Andrew off to bed, and he said nothing to remind her, instead going to peer at the long, slender jewel box the maid handed to her mistress. "This just came for you, miss," the girl said, suppressed excitement in her voice. "The duke's footman delivered it."

"The duke!" Betsy took the box and opened it. Inside lay a simple gold chain with a dainty gold heart locket decorated with a diamond chip. "Oh, my," breathed Betsy. She looked at the card. It read simply, "Best wishes, L." She smiled and looked to her grandmother, her eyes full of hope.

Mrs. Long merely shook her head.

True to her word, Lady Browning had turned the duke's townhouse into a microcosm of the Vauxhall pleasure gardens. Potted palms and ferns abounded. Rose-colored silk made a delicate tent above the great room, and in one corner, as promised, sat a fountain surrounded by gaily colored Chinese lanterns and potted palms. Candelabra stood everywhere, decorated with pink bows and roses. "Oh, my," breathed Betsy, looking around her.

"My cousin has outdone herself," said Littlefield, at her side.

"It is beautiful. Thank you."

"You must thank Maddy," said the duke.

"But I must thank you for lending us the use of your house," said Betsy. She fingered the locket at her throat and turned suddenly shy. "And for this necklace," she added, blushing.

"The veriest nothing," said the duke. "I am glad it pleases you. Who gave you the flowers?"

"Sir Harry sent the gardenia," said Betsy.

Littlefield grinned. "Good old Sir Harry. And the roses?"

"They are from Lord Amhearst."

Littlefield's grin shrunk. "Humph," he said. "Well, I think I hear our first guests at the door. We had best form our receiving line."

It seemed to Betsy that a thousand new faces swam past her on their way to the

ballroom. She searched the line for Lady
Hyacinth, hoping her friend would be present to lend her support, but saw no sign
of her.

Next to her, the duke was smiling stiffly.
Was something wrong? He did not seem
inordinately pleased. She stole a look at
Lady Browning, who was smiling graciously and holding out her hand to another arrival. And she noticed her ladyship
steal a surreptitious glance at the end of
the line of guests. Was she looking for
someone in particular?

Lord Amhearst strolled into sight, plac-
ing himself at the end of the line. Good,
thought Betsy. At least here is someone I
know besides Sir Harry and the duke and
Lady Browning

The line continued to move, and at last
Lord Amhearst stood before them. "Am-
hearst! Where is your mother? And the
Flower?" demanded the duke.

"Lady Manchester's rout," said Lord Amhearst. He looked apologetically at Betsy.

"I wasn't aware Lady Manchester was
holding a rout tonight," said Lady Browning.

Lord Amhearst looked grim. "It was
rather impromptu."

"Never mind," said Lady Browning with
forced gaiety. "I am sure they will not

have half so good a time at the Manchesters' rout as they would have had at our ball."

"Have you saved me a waltz?" Amhearst asked Betsy.

"I most certainly have," she said. "And I have saved one for the duke as well," she added.

"And what of Sir Harry?" teased the earl. "I know he is planning on dancing with you."

"I have saved him the Scotch reel."

"A very clever plan," approved his lordship. "That will leave him too winded to talk."

Littlefield frowned at his friend and suggested they repair to the ballroom.

Lady Browning looked longingly at the stairs, as if she hoped more guests would materialize, then said, "Yes, I suppose we may safely do so."

The Duke of Littlefield led Betsy out for the opening dance. Lord Browning, a genial man who was every bit as sociable as his wife, partnered her for the quadrille. They had no sooner come off the floor when his wife appeared with a new dance partner.

Then the Scotch reel was announced, and Sir Harry came to collect her. "Well,

Miss Brightham, are you enjoying your-self?" he asked.

"Oh, quite," she said. "I feel a little like Cinderella."

A more imaginative man might have made reference to Prince Charming, but Sir Harry merely smiled and observed that she looked very nice wearing the flower he had sent.

"It is lovely," she said. "Thank you."

"Not at all, not at all," he said genially, and smiled beneficently on her as they took their places for the dance. Before the reel was half over, his smile had changed to a grimace of determination, and the sweat was pouring down his face. At the end of the dance, he mopped his brow, accepted her compliments on his lightness of foot, and informed her that she looked very heated. "Perhaps you would care for some punch?" he suggested.

"That would be nice," agreed Betsy. She watched him go and smiled. Sir Harry really was a nice man, she thought. It was a pity she felt nothing for him.

Sir Harry was taking two cups of punch from a footman when he encountered the duke. "Ah, Bacon. How goes it?" asked Littlefield.

"Miss Brightham is thirsty, and I am fetching her some punch," Bacon informed him. "Curst nice female. Cannot thank you enough for putting me onto her," he continued. "She told me I am an excellent dancer. I think that a good sign, don't you?"

Littlefield shrugged. "She was, most likely, being polite," he said discouragingly.

"I think she rather likes me," continued Sir Harry. "I am going to offer for her soon, before old Amhearst can steal a march on me."

"There's no rush," said Littlefield, perversely discouraging what he had once sought. "Amhearst will never offer for her. I am sure the field is clear, so best take your time."

"I don't know," said Sir Harry. "Pretty little thing like that. And with money. No sense waiting till some other man swoops her off from right under my nose." He looked to where Betsy sat perched on a gilt-edged chair. "Look at that. Pretty as a painting."

Littlefield looked. "She is," he had to agree.

Seeing Lady Browning and another woman not far away, Betsy decided to go tell her friend what a wonderful time she was having. Coming up behind her ladyship and the woman, she arrived in time to hear the other lady say, "Why you would not listen to your dearest friend, I cannot guess. Did I not tell you how it would be? Even you cannot change the fact that the girl is a nobody."

"She is hardly a nobody when the Duke of Littlefield offers his home for her come-out ball," said Lady Browning stiffly.

"We all know why he does that," said the other woman. She surveyed the room. "I think, all things considered, you have done well in getting the crowd you have." As if feeling Betsy's eyes on her, the woman turned around and gave a start. "Miss Brightham," she managed. "How you startled me! Are you enjoying your ball?"

Betsy had been until now. She blinked back tears, determined to pretend she had not heard the woman's words. "Yes, very much," she managed. "Everyone has been so kind to me." These last words choked her, and she fled out the nearest door and onto the balcony.

"Oh, dear," fretted Lady Browning. "Now look what you have done," she accused her friend.

The woman shrugged. "I only spoke the truth."

Lord Amhearst had seen Betsy's flight

to the balcony, and he followed her. "Miss Brightham?" he said gently, stepping out and closing the door behind him. "Has something happened to upset you?"

The stooping shoulders straightened, and from the way her arms moved, he could tell she was brushing away tears. She shook her head. "No. I am fine, I assure you," she said in a wobbly voice. She gripped the rail and added, "It was getting rather stuffy inside, so I came out for some fresh air."

"It does get rather stuffy at these affairs," he said. He came to stand in back of her and put his hands on her shoulders. "Miss Brightham," he murmured.

He got no further, for Lady Browning chose that moment to join them on the balcony. "My dear. You mustn't mind that wicked creature. She is a malicious gossip."

"She only said what is true," said Betsy.

"Nonsense," said her ladyship bracingly. "What does she know? Oh, this is all my fault. I chose a bad night for your ball. Can you ever forgive me?"

Betsy turned. "Forgive you? More like, can I ever thank you! Oh, I only hope I have not ruined you socially," she ended on a sob.

"Nonsense," said Lady Browning. "Now. The night is not over. We have plenty of guests who are all enjoying themselves quite well, and I propose we go back inside and do the same."

Betsy sniffed, and Lord Amhearst offered her his handkerchief. "Thank you," she said, and looked at each of them gratefully. "Both of you," she added.

Back inside, Betsy tried to set aside the words she had overheard and enjoy her ball. She waltzed with Lord Amhearst, and the duke partnered her in the quadrille, then fetched her some supper.

"You are hardly eating," Littlefield observed.

"I am not very hungry," confessed Betsy.

"Excitement," said the duke sagely. "Poor Amhearst's sister could barely converse at her come-out ball."

"Was it well-attended?" asked Betsy.

"A veritable crush," said Littlefield. "There was barely room to move out on the floor."

Betsy looked at the dancers as they moved freely about the sparsely populated ballroom floor and sighed.

The duke followed her gaze and cleared his throat. "Of course, their ballroom is much smaller than this one."

"There is no need to pretend. I know my come-out ball is not a great success," said Betsy in a small voice.

"Nonsense," said Littlefield. "I am here. The Brownings are here. Our grandmothers are here. Amhearst and old Bacon are here."

"All my true friends," Betsy mused, and the duke seemed to squirm.

"Bacon intends to offer for you," he said.

"And would you like that?" asked Betsy.

"That is why you came to London, is it not?" countered the duke. "To make a fine match?" He studied her as he said it.

"It is why my grandmother brought me," hedged Betsy.

"Well, then. You should be happy," he snapped. "Come. If you are not going to eat, then we may as well dance." He pulled her out onto the floor, and they joined the waltzing couples. It seemed to Betsy, he held her closer than necessary, but as she found the sensation most pleasant she said nothing. She was sure he brushed her hair with his cheek. "That curst flower," he muttered. "It is enough to make me sneeze."

The music ended, and the duke pulled away from her as if trying to free himself from fetters. "I suppose my cousin has any number of fools waiting to dance with you, so I shall take you to her."

Betsy said nothing, only let the duke

lead her back to Lady Browning, who smiled and told him it was about time he quit monopolizing Betsy. "I still have a number of eligible young men to introduce to her. You she can see anytime."

He bowed and stalked off. Betsy watched him and sighed. "How much longer will this affair last?" she asked.

"Not nearly long enough for all I intend to do," said Lady Browning with determination. "Now, come. I want to present you to a gentleman who has been waiting for an introduction this past hour."

At last the ball ended. If Betsy was less than enthusiastic about the evening, her grandmother wrote it off to exhaustion. "I am sure I cannot remember when I have enjoyed myself so much," Mrs. Long said to Mrs. Whitworth. "It does take one back, does it not?"

Mrs. Whitworth smiled. "It does," she agreed. She looked at Betsy, quiet in her corner of the carriage, and her smile faded.

The following day, Sir Harry called. He asked to speak to Mrs. Long, and was closeted with her in the library for some time.

When they emerged, both were smiling. Mrs. Long had Sir Harry shown into the drawing room, then sent a servant to fetch Betsy there.

Betsy was, at first, surprised to enter the drawing room and find only Sir Harry present. But it didn't take more than a few seconds for her to realize why they had been left alone together.

"Ah, my dear Miss Brightham," said Sir Harry, coming to take her hand and lead her to the sofa. "I hope I may call you my dear Miss Brightham. In fact . . ." Here he snatched a sofa cushion and threw it on the floor, lowering himself with a grunt to kneel on it. "I hope I may call you my future bride. Would you do me the honor of—"

"Oh, no!" gasped Betsy, jumping up. "That is, oh, I know what a great honor you do me, but I am afraid I must decline."

Sir Harry looked nonplussed. "Miss Brightham," he began.

"I am afraid my heart already belongs to another," she said.

"Amhearst," growled Sir Harry. "Has he offered yet?"

"Why, no, but . . ."

"And he won't," said Sir Harry firmly. "The fellow is a sad rattle. He would make you a miserable husband. But I—I would be loyal. You would have your very own Park Phaeton and all the gowns you want.''

''Oh, Sir Harry, please,'' interrupted Betsy. ''I know you will make some fortunate female a most excellent husband. Unfortunately, that female is not me. Now, you must excuse me.''

She rose from the sofa and left the room, Sir Harry Bacon staring after her in shocked disbelief.

Mrs. Long hovered outside the drawing-room door, ready to rush in and offer her congratulations to the newly betrothed couple. She opened her mouth to speak when her granddaughter came rushing out but shut it again, immediately seeing that things had not gone according to plan. ''Betsy!'' she managed as Betsy rushed up the stairs. Sir Harry now came out of the room wearing a very long face. ''Sir Harry?'' she asked.

Sir Harry only shook his head and said, ''M'mother won't be happy.''

No sooner had Sir Harry left when Lord Amhearst called to visit. ''Oh, dear,'' fretted Mrs. Long. ''I am afraid Betsy has rushed off to her room. But perhaps she will come down and see you.''

''Please don't disturb her if she is feeling unwell,'' said his lordship politely.

"She must be to turn down Sir Harry," muttered Mrs. Long.

The look of extreme interest on Lord Amhearst's face caused her to clamp her lips shut.

He smiled and said, "If you would be so good as to tell her I called. I shall wait and pay my respects again tomorrow."

"Certainly," said Mrs. Long. Lord Amhearst took his leave, and she watched him go, a thoughtful expression on her face. "Perhaps," she said, "perhaps."

Twelve

Lady Browning called the following day. "I came to make sure you planned to attend Lady Darrell's rout this evening," she told Betsy.

"I think not," said Betsy.

"Now, Betsy dear," said her grandmama, "I am sure Lord Amhearst would be disappointed not to find you there."

"I am sure I would be disappointed if she did not accompany Charles and me," put in her ladyship.

Betsy smiled. "Dear friend. Do not think to fool me into believing your life was friendless before the duke forced my company upon you."

"It may not have been friendless, but it was certainly dull," insisted Lady Browning. "Please come. Lionel will be there," she added.

Betsy shrugged nonchalantly. "I am sure he will enjoy himself far more then, if I am not."

"On the contrary," corrected her ladyship. "I think he will be like a bear with a sore paw if you are not present. And I shall certainly be in the mopes. Oh, please come."

"You must go," added her grandmother firmly. "After all, this is why we came to London, to launch you in society."

Betsy looked to Mrs. Whitworth, hoping to find an ally. "They are right, child," she said.

"Very well," said Betsy. "But I do not relish it."

As she moved through Lady Darrell's crowded rooms that night, Betsy told herself she had been right. She recognized a few faces from her ball, and some of the guests talked with her, but for the most part she felt like an outsider. Until she saw Lord Amhearst and his mother and sister come in.

Lady Hyacinth saw her and, smiling, hurried across the room. "Oh, I am so glad you are here," she said. "I wanted so very much to attend your ball, but Mama insisted we go to Lady Manchester's rout."

"Ah, well," said Betsy, and then couldn't help asking, "Was it lovely?"

"It was a crush," said Lady Hyacinth. "There were so many people milling about, I vow I felt suffocated." This didn't seem to be the thing to say, for it made Betsy look positively despondent. "I am sure the decorations were not half so fine as yours," added Lady Hyacinth.

"It was very beautiful," admitted Betsy. She looked around her. "And my, what a crowd Lady Darrell has tonight! Do you know all these people?"

"Heavens, no!" said Lady Hyacinth. "That is why I was so very glad to see you."

"Hyacinth, dear. There you are," said her Mama. "Good evening, Miss Brightham."

"Lady Amhearst," said Betsy, curtsying.

"Hyacinth. Lady Darrell has a young man who is dying to meet you. You will excuse us?" she said to Betsy.

"Of course," said Betsy. She watched sadly as Lady Amhearst led her friend away. But she was not alone long before Lady Browning appeared with another young woman in tow.

"I know you will enjoy talking with Miss Brightham," she was saying.

Until your mama comes and snatches you away, thought Betsy miserably. She forced her lips into a smile. It was going to be a long evening.

It seemed to Littlefield that he had barely gotten in the door before Lord Amhearst had cornered him. He looked at Betsy, standing across the room with his cousin and some other female, smiling politely and furtively scanning the room. Was she looking for him?

"I told you the Brightham wouldn't have old Bacon," crowed Lord Amhearst. "Although I must say, you put out a good effort."

"The bet was not for whether or not she would have him but whether or not he would offer for her," said Littlefield stiffly.

"Stone cold sober," added Amhearst. "But we will never know whether he was sober or not. I suppose we can ask him. Ah, well. No matter. I shall pay up and not grouse, for our little wager has made the season most enjoyable. And I must admit, I am surprised that Bacon would offer for a female with neither title nor money."

The young lady who had come up to stand at Lord Amhearst's elbow backed quickly away, unseen, then hurried to the opposite side of the room to speak to Betsy.

"I shall come round tomorrow and pay up," said Lord Amhearst genially.

"Excellent," said Littlefield, and walked off, leaving his friend to wonder why he seemed so remote.

Littlefield was making his way to Betsy

when he was waylaid by Lord Lyon. "I hear old Amhearst lost his wager with you," said the Lion heartily.

"It was a ridiculous wager in the first place," snapped Littlefield.

"Yes, you had the luck of the devil himself. I vow, Littlefield, soon none of us will wish to wager with you at all, for you seem to be very lucky these days." Lord Lyon shook his head. "Ah, well, that ends the ballroom sport for the season, and I am back to Boodle's, I assure you."

"Yes, well, that is the best place for wagers anyway," said the duke, and excused himself.

Lord Lyon watched the Duke of Littlefield make his way to where Miss Brightham stood with Lady Hyacinth and shook his head. "Odd," he said to himself.

Littlefield noticed that Elizabeth seemed very pale. She normally greeted him with friendliness, no, open admiration in her eyes. Right now she regarded him with haughty disdain. Something was amiss. "Good evening, Lady Hyacinth," he said kindly, bowing over the girl's hand. He turned to Elizabeth. "Elizabeth," he murmured, and smiled at her before taking her hand.

"Good evening, Your Grace," she replied stiffly. "I hope you are enjoying yourself."

"Why, now that I have seen you I am," he replied gallantly. She did not smile. "Are you feeling quite well?" he enquired politely.

"I am afraid not," she said.

"It is close in here," he observed. "Perhaps some punch would help."

A wicked smile lit her face. "Perhaps it would," she agreed, her voice velvet.

Littlefield stopped a passing footman and scooped a cup of punch from his tray, then handed it to Betsy.

Smiling at him, she took the cup and threw its contents on his chest.

His eyes widened in shock. He heard Lady Hyacinth gasp, caught a glimpse of his cousin hiding a mischievous smile behind her fan, heard the soft murmur of voices as word raced round the room of what Miss Brightham had just done to the Duke of Littlefield.

"Thank you for the punch," she said sweetly. "I feel so much better." She turned to Lady Browning, who had just joined them. "If it is not too much trouble, I should like to go home now."

"Certainly, dearest," said her ladyship. "I never liked that brown coat by half," she informed Littlefield, then swept Betsy off.

Betsy managed to keep her countenance until Lady Browning and her husband had her safely inside their carriage. Then the tears spilled. "My dear, what has happened?" asked Lady Browning, putting an arm around Betsy.

"It was all for a wager," sobbed Betsy.

"Oh, dear," said Lord Browning, and he and his lady exchanged knowing looks.

"Lady Hyacinth overheard her brother and the duke talking."

"Bad ton," said Lord Browning.

"Wicked," snapped her ladyship. "There now, dear, don't cry. Men are beasts, and well we all know it." Here she gave her husband a look which declared him guilty by association. "They are always making absurd wagers, and no lady who is a true lady would pay any regard to such nonsense. Come now, you must try to compose yourself before we get you home. It would never do to have your grandmama see you like this."

"I want to leave London," wailed Betsy.

"Well, you cannot," said Lady Browning firmly. "To run away would be the worst thing you could possibly do."

"I don't belong here. Oh, don't you see. I simply do not belong."

"You do not belong? Was it you who made such a ridiculous wager?" retorted her ladyship.

Betsy sniffed. "No," she said weakly.

"Well, then. I think my cousin should be the one planning to leave town with a red face."

"But I poured punch on him," Betsy reminded her.

Her ladyship smiled, her brown eyes twinkling. "And how lovely he looks in ratafia," she murmured.

The Duke of Littlefield was, at that moment, in his carriage on his way home. Like a man with a sore tooth, who must continue to poke at it, he touched a finger to his coat, then pulled it away in disgust. What could have prompted such bizarre behavior? Did the female have a canker on the brain? He would call tomorrow and give her the opportunity to grovel and beg forgiveness.

He shouldn't. He knew he shouldn't. After all, he was the Duke of Littlefield. And who was she?

"She is Lord Slocomb's daughter?" Lady Browning repeated, stunned, and fell back against the sofa cushions.

Mrs. Long nodded. "The duke advised

her to tell no one of her first father. As he was killed in a gambling hell, I am sure the duke thought it would be more of an embarrassment than a help to Betsy."

Lady Browning rolled her eyes. "And I suppose she is not without expectations."

"Modest ones," admitted Mrs. Long, and blushed guiltily as Mrs. Whitworth stared at her in amazement.

Lady Browning looked at Betsy triumphantly. "Now, never say you don't belong. You are one of us. And I intend to make sure everyone of my acquaintance knows it." She smiled at Mrs. Long. "I am so glad we had this little talk."

"Thank you for bringing our poor lamb home," said Mrs. Long. "Oh, when I think of it!"

"Now, don't you worry about my cousin," said Lady Browning. "He will be well served for his tricks, for I promise you, he will have put his foot in parson's mousetrap before the next season has begun." Here she gave Betsy a playful tap with her fan, and Mrs. Long smiled.

Betsy saw no humor in the remark. Obviously Lady Browning knew something she did not. Obviously the duke had been interested in another lady all along, and she really was nothing more to him than a wager.

Fresh tears sprang to her eyes, and her grandmother, seeing them, said, "Now, I think what we need is to get you to bed, my girl. It has been an exhausting night, and everything will look better in the morning, I assure you."

Betsy knew things would neither look nor be better in the morning, but she allowed herself to be bustled off to her room and the tender ministrations of her maid.

The morning brought the Duke of Littlefield. The butler showed him into the drawing room to wait, and there he encountered Mrs. Long.

She was polite but distant in her greeting, and although it had been her granddaughter and not himself who had gone about pouring punch on people the night before, the duke graciously overlooked her lack of warmth. "Did you wish to see Betsy, Your Grace?" asked Mrs. Long.

"Yes, I did," he said, resorting to hauteur.

"In that case, I shall leave you, for I am sure my granddaughter will wish to have a word with you alone."

She left the room, and the duke concluded that Elizabeth was too embarrassed over her behavior to make her apology in front of her grandmother.

Betsy entered the room. She brought with her no welcoming look for the Duke of Littlefield. Nor did she appear the least penitent. "I hope you are feeling better," said Littlefield stiffly. "Have you recovered from whatever aberration caused you to behave so strangely last night?"

Betsy raised an eyebrow. "Aberration? Yes," she said thoughtfully. "It must have been an aberration which caused me to become upset when I learned I was no more to you than a wager."

The duke felt a sudden draining of blood from his face.

"What a fool I was!" declared Betsy. "My grandmama told me you only danced attendance on me because Mrs. Whitworth forced you to. But I could not believe it, did not wish to believe it. I thought you had come to care. How wrong I was! I was not even an obligation. I was only . . . sport," she choked.

"Elizabeth," began the duke.

"I thought you were kind. And noble," Betsy continued, her voice rising with increased pain. "Truly noble. So noble you did not care that I was a nobody. But you care for nothing and no one—except yourself. Well now, you have won your wager, and you may take yourself off and go to . . . the devil!" With that she turned

and ran from the room, leaving a shocked
Duke of Littlefield alone with his con-
science.

Thirteen

Lady Amhearst, on hearing of her son's ungentlemanly behavior, was both shocked and disgusted. However, she was not so much so that her daughter could stir her to take any action on Miss Brightham's behalf. "Our association with that unhappy young lady can do you no good," she said firmly. "Wherever she goes there is a scene. Only remember how she made her appearance at Almack's! And now this contretemps last night. Then think of her family."

"They are a little eccentric," admitted Lady Hyacinth.

"They are an embarrassment. My dear child, the nobility only accepts eccentricity among themselves. If she had any real claim to nobility, perhaps she could be forgiven. But really, who is she?" Lady Amhearst shook her head. "No, I am afraid the poor thing is doomed to a destiny far different from yours."

Lady Hyacinth sighed. "Poor Miss Bright-ham," she said.

The duke left his grandmother's house and set off for Tattersall's, where he normally would have happily idled away a few hours. Tattersall's was flat. He thought of going to Angelo's Haymarket Room, for he was definitely in the mood to run someone through with a sword. Unfortunately, Angelo did not allow gentlemen to vent their spleen quite so thoroughly. He settled for going to Jackson's and, after an hour of vigorous boxing, felt only mildly better.

Curse the wretched chit! he thought as he climbed atop his curricle. She was quite ruining his day. Her words still stung his ears. Was he really such a beast?

To reassure himself that he was not, he drove to Brooks's. It was a gray spring day, and he was sure the drizzle would have driven many of his cronies to that gambling haven to wile away the tedious afternoon hours. He was not mistaken. He found Lord Amhearst and Lord Lyon playing picquet, Sir Harry Bacon idly watching. "Hullo, Littlefield," said Bacon. "I suppose I should call you out or something for making an ass of me, but I fear you are too good both with sword and pistol."

Littlefield clapped him on the shoulder. "You are a good sport," he said. "At any rate, she would have made you a fine wife."

"Not with that family of hers. But a mistress, yes."

Littlefield frowned at this.

"Too late, old fellow," said Lord Amhearst, tossing out a card. "I have already instructed Farrington to pop round this afternoon."

"Farrington?" said the duke sharply.

"He is acting as love monger for me," said the earl. "I don't know whether she'll have a go at it or not, being a vicar's stepdaughter, but . . ."

"What!" roared the duke. He slammed both hands on the table and towered over his startled friend. "Are you tired of your life on this earth?"

His friend looked at him as if he'd run mad. "What the devil's the matter with you?" he stammered. "I mean to take good care of the girl."

"You had best send a note to Farrington telling him you have changed your mind," said the duke. "Else I shall have to end our friendship by ending your life."

Lord Amhearst's eyes widened. "You?

You want to set her up? Why did you not say so?"

"Curse it all," roared the duke. "I don't want to set her up. I want to marry her!" He straightened, looking as surprised as his friends. Then he smiled and nodded. "Yes. I do."

"If that don't beat the dutch!" exclaimed Lord Amhearst. "I should have known. Well, and did I not say it? Only a man in love would tolerate children and mongrels running through his house."

Grinning foolishly, the duke went home to plan his strategy for winning the heart of Miss Elizabeth Brightham. He found Whitey lying before the drawing-room hearth chewing on a sofa cushion. "Give me that!" he snapped, and grabbed the cushion.

Whitey thought this game great fun, snarled, and pulled the other end of the cushion. "Give me that you wretched cur!" growled the duke and yanked.

There was a rending of fabric, followed by a whirlwind of feathers. Whitey jumped at a feather and yapped excitedly, and the duke bellowed for his butler. He looked at the offending animal, happily chasing feathers. "I suppose once I marry her I shall have to suffer both you and Andrew under my roof frequently," he told the animal.

Whitey wagged his tail.

Ignoring him, and the feathers, the duke went to the mantel and picked up the invitations that had been placed there for his inspection. A dinner invitation from Lady Browning caught his interest. "I know you shan't fail me," her ladyship had written. "To attend is the least you can do for the daughter of the viscount, Lord Slocomb. I am sure you will remember him, the man who was killed in a gaming hell?"

Gaming hell . . . daughter . . . The duke felt a sudden need to sit down.

There were fourteen for dinner at Lady Browning's. In addition to himself, his cousins, and Elizabeth and her grandmama, Littlefield saw Lady Cowper and her husband had been produced, as well as Lord Palmerston. His cousin had also invited that conceited dandy, Sir Derek Chatterly, who was already monopolizing Elizabeth in conversation as they waited for the summons to the dining room. Littlefield gave a mental snort. He knew for a fact that the fellow padded his legs.

The duke continued to number the other guests. There was a gouty middle-aged rake and a favorite ton hostess with her husband and daughter. He supposed he would have to do the pretty with the daughter sometime this evening. And here came his paternal grandmother.

"Lionel," she greeted him. "What a naughty boy you are! Pretending that sweet young lady had no noble blood in her. If you had only told me at the first, you would have made things so much easier for everyone. She seems a perfectly nice young woman."

"She is," said Littlefield, looking wistfully to where Elizabeth stood. Why must she smile at the jackanapes as if she were interested in him? She would only encourage him.

Dinner was announced, and the stately procession into the dining room began. For the first time, the Duke of Littlefield cursed his high estate, for it made him unable to lead Elizabeth in to dinner and kept him separated from her the entire meal.

After dinner, the ladies left for the drawing room, and Littlefield vowed the minute the gentlemen followed he would get a seat next to her.

True to his vow, he was able to displace his cousin and secure a seat next to Elizabeth. "Why did you not tell me your father was nobility?" he demanded.

"You told me not to mention my first father," she replied stiffly.

The duke gave an impatient hiss. "If he was nobility," he began.

"He might be forgiven anything?" interrupted Betsy.

"Yes," said the duke, his tone decidedly defensive. "Especially if he has been kind enough to procure vouchers to Almack's, house a mongrel dog, and drag a child about Vauxhall."

"I am told a gentleman will go to great lengths to win a wager," said Betsy airily. The duke glared threateningly at her, but she continued, unafraid, "Ah, how wonderful to be one of the upper ten thousand, to be allowed to behave in the most ignoble fashion and still call oneself nobility. It is rather like spending the day shoveling manure, then putting on a fine coat and calling yourself clean, is it not? But then, why do I ask you? What would you know of such things?" With that, she turned her shoulder on him, intending to give her attention to the young lady on her other side who was trying to look as if she had heard nothing.

"Miss Brightham," said Littlefield sternly.

She looked haughtily over her shoulder at him. "I am quite finished speaking with you," she informed him. "In fact, I had much rather speak with the lowest gardener on your estate than with your noble self." And to emphasize her point, she removed herself to another seat, leaving the duke red-faced and angry.

He spent the rest of the evening watching her flirt shamelessly with Sir Derek who, Littlefield knew, had no more than thirty thousand pounds per annum. Fine! Let him have her. Littlefield would send them Whitey for a wedding gift.

As soon as possible he took his leave, sarcastically thanking his cousin for a delightful evening.

"I think it was most entertaining," she said amiably. "I would not wait too long to offer for her, Lionel. Absence does make the heart grow fonder, but not always for the absent one."

Littlefield snatched his hat and gloves from the butler and left, vowing the only offer Miss Elizabeth Brightham would get from him was to dance at her engagement ball. *Which* could be held somewhere other than Littlefield House!

Fourteen

Although her paternal grandmother still did not acknowledge her, the rest of society was more willing to accept the Hon. Elizabeth Brightham, especially the young men, who had heard she had some sort of inheritance waiting for her on her twenty-first birthday. Sir Derek seemed to be the suitor she favored most, and during the two weeks following Lady Browning's dinner party, the two were seen frequently together.

It appeared to Littlefield that whenever he glanced their way, whether at the opera or at a ball, she was flirting determinedly with the worthless fellow. Bah! Let him have her, thought the duke. She was a curst nuisance.

"Yes, yes," agreed Lord Amhearst. "A veritable thorn in the flesh. Which means you will be glad to hear that Chatterly means to offer for her."

"What! He has known her little more than a fortnight."

"That is enough when Cupid's arrow strikes," said Amhearst with a shrug. "She is a pleasing little thing."

Littlefield frowned.

His friend slapped him on the back. "Buck up, old fellow. You cannot win every battle."

The only answer Lord Amhearst received from the duke was a growl.

Lady Browning called at Mrs. Whitworth's house to see Miss Brightham.

"Dear Lady Browning," enthused Mrs. Long. "I know Betsy will be so happy you have called. She is having a little lie-down, but I will have her got up."

"Oh, pray, don't do that on my account," said Lady Browning.

"I know she will want to see you. In fact, I am sure it will do her good. She has not been quite herself these past few days," confided Mrs. Long. She shook her head. "I am afraid that wretched duke has quite broken her heart."

"He has not called?"

Mrs. Long shook her head. "Ah, well," she said philosophically. "Sir Derek seems a nice young man. And such a fine dresser!"

"Yes," said her ladyship, unimpressed.

"I am sure he means to offer for Betsy."

"My cousin had best stir himself then," observed her ladyship.

At that moment, Johnston arrived, announcing that Sir Derek had come to have a word with Mrs. Long.

"Oh, my," said Mrs. Long, her voice vibrating with excitement. "I pray you will excuse me?"

"Of course," murmured Lady Browning. "I shall be on my way."

"Tell Sir Derek I shall be happy to see him in the library," instructed Mrs. Long. "And see that my granddaughter is sent for immediately."

"Very good, madam," said the butler, and withdrew.

Sir Derek was ensconced in the library, and Mrs. Long was just bidding Lady Browning farewell when the sound of raised voices drifted down from the stairs. A moment later, Andrew came running down them, pursued by Betsy's abigail.

He ran to hide behind Lady Browning's skirts and the maid caught herself midway down the stairs and bobbed an embarrassed curtsy.

"Whatever is going on here?" demanded Mrs. Long.

"I caught Master Andrew with Miss Betsy's journal," accused the maid.

"Andrew!" gasped his grandmama in shock. "What a naughty boy! Now, you must give me that immediately."

Andrew hugged the book to him and said, "I just want to read it. I won't ruin it."

"Andrew," said Mrs. Long firmly.

Lady Browning's face had taken on a thoughtful appearance. "Perhaps you had best see Sir Derek," she suggested to Mrs. Long. "I shall be happy to take care of Andrew." She held out her hand to Andrew. "Come, Andrew. Let's go into the drawing room."

Andrew decided that Lady Browning posed less of a threat than his grandmama, and docilely took her ladyship's hand.

"Do not think you shall go unpunished, young man," said his grandmother in ominous tones, and went into the library.

Lady Browning hurried into the drawing room. "Quickly, Andrew. Let me see the journal."

Andrew handed over the book, and her ladyship sank onto a chair and briskly turned to the last few pages. " 'I had such dreams when we first met the duke,' " she read, " 'but they were childish and silly.' " She flipped the pages. " 'I should not have talked so to him, for I know I have wounded his pride, and I fear he will never forgive me that. And I know not whether it is pride or lack of imagination which prevents me from finding a way to speak to him.' "

Lady Browning looked thoughtfully at Andrew. "The duke is a great friend of yours, is he not?" she asked.

"Oh, yes," replied Andrew cheerfully. "But we have not seen him all this week and more."

"Andrew. Do you understand the things you have read in this book?"

Andrew shook his head. "Could you explain them to me?"

"I think not," said Lady Browning. "But I know someone who can."

The Duke of Littlefield sat in his favorite leather chair in his library, staring at the wine in his glass, unaware of Whitey lying below with his head on the duke's boot. He did not hear the first time Macomber announced his visitor, and the butler had to repeat himself. "Andrew. What the devil brings the cub here?" he muttered. "He should be calling on Chatterly," he added bitterly.

"Does Your Grace wish me to send him away?" asked Macomber.

Before the duke could reply, Andrew had slipped past the butler and into the room. "Whitey!" he cried, and, dropping the book he carried, he fell on the floor to hug the dog's neck.

The duke saw the book and picked it up. "What is this?"

Andrew turned his face so the dog could lick his other cheek and said, "It is Betsy's. There are things in it I don't understand. Can you explain them to me?"

Unable to resist temptation, the duke flipped through the pages. Some of what he read made him smile and shake his head. But what he read toward the end of the book made him frown. He came to the last page, and his eyes widened as he read, "Sir Derek has told me he means to wait upon Grandmama tomorrow. And then he will press me for an answer. I fear it will have to be yes."

"We shall see about that," Littlefield said. He jumped up and began to pace.

"Can you explain to me what Betsy wrote?" asked Andrew eagerly.

"I cannot even explain it to myself," snapped Littlefield. "Here now, can you not see I am trying to think? Find James and take Whitey for a walk."

"Will the gardener find a stick for us to take to throw for Whitey?" asked Andrew.

The duke stopped in his tracks. "The gardener," he repeated. "Andrew! You are brilliant!"

"Miss Brightham," said Sir Derek. "Please say that you will make me the happiest of men."

The moment she had been dreading had come at last. Contrary to Lady Browning's predictions, the Duke of Littlefield had not been the least jealous of Sir Derek. And since she had encouraged him and flirted with him shamelessly, Betsy supposed she had no choice but to take him. "Oh dear," she said.

"Oh dear?" he repeated, stunned.

A gentle tapping at the drawing-room door caused Betsy to jump up from the sofa. "Who can that be?" she said hopefully, and called, "Come in."

The upstairs maid took a nervous step into the room. "Mrs. Long said you wasn't to be disturbed, Miss Brightham, but there is a man at the kitchen door wanting to speak with you."

"The kitchen door," echoed Sir Derek, shocked. "You disturbed Miss Brightham to tell her of some peddlar at the kitchen door?"

The girl bit her lip. "Mr. Johnston talked to the man and said I was to come fetch you directly and never mind what Mrs. Long said," she managed.

"Very well," Betsy said to the girl. "You did fine, Jane." She smiled at Sir Derek. "Please excuse me, Sir Derek. I shan't be a moment."

"But, Miss Brightham," protested Sir Derek. "Can you not give me an answer before you leave?"

But Betsy was already out the door. She hurried down the hall, hope pushing her on. Surely there could be only one man who would have the power to interrupt a proposal of marriage.

She sped into the kitchen, which was strangely deserted, only to find to her disappointment the man standing in the doorway with his back to her was only a gardener.

But wait! She looked again, hardly able to believe her eyes as the man turned, cap in hand, and looked humbly at her. "Would you speak with a lowly gardener?" asked the duke softly.

"Your Grace?"

"I wish you would call me Gabriel," he

said. "Although Beelzebub would, most likely, be more fitting."

Betsy stood rooted in the doorway, and he walked into the room.

"Will you give me a moment?" he asked.

She nodded, stepping into the room and letting the door shut behind her. "Why are you dressed like this?" she asked, taking in his mud-encrusted shirt.

"Because I realized with the way I'd been acting I had no right to come to you in fine clothes. I come to you as I really am, raw, filthy, in desperate need of civilizing." He moved to stand directly before her, then fell to one knee. "Elizabeth. Would you do me the honor of becoming my wife? Would you take this poor man and make him into someone worthy of you?"

Betsy took a step back. "You mock me, Your Grace. This is some fresh wager, meant to make me look foolish."

The duke rose. In spite of his patched clothes and dirty face, he looked every inch a duke, and every inch a man of power. "This is no wager," he said. "But I can assure you, much is at stake. My entire future, in fact."

Still, Betsy said nothing.

"My grandmother asked me to help bring you out," he continued. "She asked because I have power and position. I could have used these gifts to do you great good. Instead, I did you great mischief. If ever a man deserved to suffer for the rest of his life, it is I, but . . ."

The duke got no further. Betsy threw herself into his arms and drove her lips against his. As the gown she was wearing looked suspiciously like one she had made herself, he had no compunction about pulling her against his dirty shirt and wrapping his arms around her, returning her kiss with equal enthusiasm.

Lord Amhearst waltzed his sister around Lady Browning's ballroom floor. As they waltzed by the Duke of Littlefield and Miss Brightham, Lady Hyacinth smiled at her friend and waved white-gloved fingers in her direction. "I think they make a prodigious fine couple," she informed her brother, who merely grunted. "And," she continued, "I am so glad Miss Brightham did not wind up some man's mistress."

His lordship frowned and told her it was bad ton for a lady to talk of such things, even with her brother.

"She really is quite lovely," observed Lady Hyacinth, still not finished with the subject of Miss Brightham.

Lord Amhearst sighed. "Littlefield is a lucky dog," he said.

Lady Jersey watched the betrothed couple glide by, took a sip of punch, then said to Lady Cowper, "I never said we should not admit her to Almack's. I simply said, 'Who is she?' All you had to do, my dear, was to say, 'She is Slocomb's daughter.' "

Lady Cowper gave her friend a look which said Lady Jersey could say what she liked, but everyone knew who could really be thanked for the girl's success.

In another corner of the room, Mrs. Long and Mrs. Whitworth sat and watched their grandchildren. "Yes, indeed, a very fine match we have produced, my dear Jane," said Mrs. Long. "Who would have thought when we were girls together at Miss Marrywell's Seminary that one day we would be sitting together as old women, watching our grandchildren dance at their engagement ball."

Mrs. Whitworth smiled and nodded.

"And think how much we will be seeing of each other now," continued Mrs. Long.

"Yes," said Mrs. Whitworth unenthusiastically.

Littlefield smiled down at Betsy. "Happy?" he asked.

"Oh, yes," she said. "I only wish there were not such a crowd. I feel as if we barely have room to move."

Littlefield grinned. "I shall simply have to hold you closer to conserve space," he said, and matched his actions to his words. "You look incomparable tonight, you know."

She blushed. "Nonsense," she said. "There are a good many women here far prettier than I."

"I cannot see them," said the duke. "That is a lovely gown," he added.

"I would thank you, but as it was you who suggested both the pattern and the material, I see no need to swell your conceit," replied Betsy.

He chuckled. "I hope you have no beaded slippers lurking beneath it."

"Perhaps I do," she teased.

"Well, no matter," he said cheerfully. "A man should have a sense of humor."

"And do you now?" teased Betsy, smiling up at him.

He returned her smile and said, "I am a changed man." He lifted the gloved hand he held to his lips, kissed it, and murmured, "Bringing out Betsy has definitely served to bring out the best in me."

Sheila Rabe loves to hear from her readers. Please write to her c/o Zebra Books, 850 Third Avenue, New York, NY 10022.

ZEBRA'S REGENCY ROMANCES
DAZZLE AND DELIGHT

A BEGUILING INTRIGUE (4441, $3.99)
by Olivia Sumner

Pretty as a picture Justine Riggs cared nothing for propriety. She dressed as a boy, sat on her horse like a jockey, and pondered the stars like a scientist. But when she tried to best the handsome Quenton Fletcher, Marquess of Devon, by proving that she was the better equestrian, he would try to prove Justine's antics were pure folly. The game he had in mind was seduction — never imagining that he might lose his heart in the process!

AN INCONVENIENT ENGAGEMENT (4442, $3.99)
by Joy Reed

Rebecca Wentworth was furious when she saw her betrothed waltzing with another. So she decides to make him jealous by flirting with the handsomest man at the ball, John Collinwood, Earl of Stanford. The "wicked" nobleman knew exactly what the enticing miss was up to — and he was only too happy to play along. But as Rebecca gazed into his magnificent eyes, her errant fiancé was soon utterly forgotten!

SCANDAL'S LADY (4472, $3.99)
by Mary Kingsley

Cassandra was shocked to learn that the new Earl of Lynton was her childhood friend, Nicholas St. John. After years at sea and mixed feelings Nicholas had come home to take the family title. And although Cassandra knew her place as a governess, she could not help the thrill that went through her each time he was near. Nicholas was pleased to find that his old friend Cassandra was his new next door neighbor, but after being near her, he wondered if mere friendship would be enough . . .

HIS LORDSHIP'S REWARD (4473, $3.99)
by Carola Dunn

As the daughter of a seasoned soldier, Fanny Ingram was accustomed to the vagaries of military life and cared not a whit about matters of rank and social standing. So she certainly never foresaw her *tendre* for handsome Viscount Roworth of Kent with whom she was forced to share lodgings, while he carried out his clandestine activities on behalf of the British Army. And though good sense told Roworth to keep his distance, he couldn't stop from taking Fanny in his arms for a kiss that made all hearts equal!

Available wherever paperbacks are sold, or order direct from the Publisher. Send cover price plus 50¢ per copy for mailing and handling to Penguin USA, P.O. Box 999, c/o Dept. 17109, Bergenfield, NJ 07621. Residents of New York and Tennessee must include sales tax. DO NOT SEND CASH.

ELEGANT LOVE STILL FLOURISHES –
Wrap yourself in a Zebra Regency Romance.

A MATCHMAKER'S MATCH   (3783, $3.50/$4.50)
by Nina Porter

To save herself from a loveless marriage, Lady Psyche Veringham pretends to be a bluestocking. Resigned to spinsterhood at twenty-three, Psyche sets her keen mind to snaring a husband for her young charge, Amanda. She sets her cap for long-time bachelor, Justin St. James. This man of the world has had his fill of frothy-headed debutantes and turns the tables on Psyche. Can a bluestocking and a man about town find true love?

FIRES IN THE SNOW   (3809, $3.99/$4.99)
by Janis Laden

Because of an unhappy occurrence, Diana Ruskin knew that a secure marriage was not in her future. She was content to assist her physician father and follow in his footsteps . . . until now. After meeting Adam, Duke of Marchmaine, Diana's precise world is shattered. She would simply have to avoid the temptation of his gentle touch and stunning physique – and by doing so break her own heart!

FIRST SEASON   (3810, $3.50/$4.50)
by Anne Baldwin

When country heiress Laetitia Biddle arrives in London for the Season, she harbors dreams of triumph and applause. Instead, she becomes the laughingstock of drawing rooms and ballrooms, alike. This headstrong miss blames the rakish Lord Wakeford for her miserable debut, and she vows to rise above her many faux pas. Vowing to become an Original, Letty proves that she's more than a match for this eligible, seasoned Lord.

AN UNCOMMON INTRIGUE   (3701, $3.99/$4.99)
by Georgina Devon

Miss Mary Elizabeth Sinclair was rather startled when the British Home Office employed her as a spy. Posing as "Tasha," an exotic fortune-teller, she expected to encounter unforeseen dangers. However, nothing could have prepared her for Lord Eric Stewart, her dashing and infuriating partner. Giving her heart to this haughty rogue would be the most reckless hazard of all.

A MADDENING MINX   (3702, $3.50/$4.50)
by Mary Kingsley

After a curricle accident, Miss Sarah Chadwick is literally thrust into the arms of Philip Thornton. While other women shy away from Thornton's eyepatch and aloof exterior, Sarah finds herself drawn to discover why this man is physically and emotionally scarred.

Available wherever paperbacks are sold, or order direct from the Publisher. Send cover price plus 50¢ per copy for mailing and handling to Penguin USA, P.O. Box 999, c/o Dept. 17109, Bergenfield, NJ 07621. Residents of New York and Tennessee must include sales tax. DO NOT SEND CASH.

TODAY'S HOTTEST READS
ARE TOMORROW'S SUPERSTARS

VICTORY'S WOMAN   (4484, $4.50)
by Gretchen Genet
Andrew — the carefree soldier who sought glory on the battlefield,
and returned a shattered man . . . Niall — the legandary frontiers-
man and a former Shawnee captive, tormented by his past . . .
Roger — the troubled youth, who would rise up to claim a shocking legacy . . . and Clarice — the passionate beauty bound by one
man, and hopelessly in love with another. Set against the back-
drop of the American revolution, three men fight for their
heritage — and one woman is destined to change all their lives forever!

FORBIDDEN   (4488, $4.99)
by Jo Beverley
While fleeing from her brothers, who are attempting to sell her
into a loveless marriage, Serena Riverton accepts a carriage ride
from a stranger — who is the handsomest man she has ever seen.
Lord Middlethorpe, himself, is actually contemplating marriage
to a dull daughter of the aristocracy, when he encounters the
breathtaking Serena. She arouses him as no woman ever has. And
after a night of thrilling intimacy — a forbidden liaison — Serena
must choose between a lady's place and a woman's passion!

WINDS OF DESTINY   (4489, $4.99)
by Victoria Thompson
Becky Tate is a half-breed outcast — branded by her Comanche
heritage. Then she meets a rugged stranger who awakens her
heart to the magic and mystery of passion. Hiding a desperate
past, Texas Ranger Clint Masterson has ridden into cattle country
to bring peace to a divided land. But a greater battle rages inside
him when he dares to desire the beautiful Becky!

WILDEST HEART   (4456, $4.99)
by Virginia Brown
Maggie Malone had come to cattle country to forge her future as
a healer. Now she was faced by Devon Conrad, an outlaw
wounded body and soul by his shadowy past . . . whose eyes
blazed with fury even as his burning caress sent her spiraling with
desire. They came together in a Texas town about to explode in sin
and scandal. Danger was their destiny — and there was nothing
they wouldn't dare for love!

*Available wherever paperbacks are sold, or order direct from the
Publisher. Send cover price plus 50¢ per copy for mailing and
handling to Penguin USA, P.O. Box 999, c/o Dept. 17109,
Bergenfield, NJ 07621. Residents of New York and Tennessee
must include sales tax. DO NOT SEND CASH.*